Also by Amie Stuart

Make U Sweat

Nailed

"Kink" in Built

Hands On

Hittin' It

AMIE STUART

APHRODISIA
KENSINGTON BOOKS
http://www.kensingtonbooks.com

APHRODISIA BOOKS are published by

Kensington Publishing Corp.
850 Third Avenue
New York, NY 10022

Copyright © 2009 by Amie Stuart

All rights reserved. No part of this book may be reproduced in any form or by any means without the prior written consent of the Publisher, excepting brief quotes used in reviews.

All Kensington Titles, Imprints, and Distributed Lines are available at special quantity discounts for bulk purchases for sales promotions, premiums, fund-raising, and educational or institutional use.

Special book excerpts or customized printings can also be created to fit specific needs. For details, write or phone the office of the Kensington special sales manager: Kensington Publishing Corp., 850 Third Avenue, New York, NY 10022, attn: Special Sales Department, Phone: 1-800-221-2647.

Aphrodisia and the A logo Reg. U.S. Pat & TM Off.

ISBN-13: 978-0-7582-2856-7
ISBN-10: 0-7582-2856-2

First Kensington Trade Paperback Printing: March 2009

10 9 8 7 6 5 4 3 2 1

Printed in the United States of America

ACKNOWLEDGMENTS

I know it probably seems like I thank the same folks over and over again, but honestly, there's no way I could do what I do without them. So, again, in no particular order... Pamela Britton, Raine Weaver, Denise McDonald, Tanya T. Holmes, Michelle Miles, Lynn Matherly, Jackie Barbosa, Emma Petersen, Kim Terry, Bailey Stewart, and my NAS(ty) girls—Shelli, Feisty & Karen.

This one's for the girls.

SCREWED

Will and Sabrina

1

"Hey! What's your name?"

To his friends and family, he was Will; to everyone else, he was God, as in "Please God, don't kill me."

To his ex-girlfriend, he was, "You impotent bastard."

Whatever.

His driver's license said he was William Tanner Collier of Oklahoma City. But to this man, he was, "Roy . . . Roy Rogers."

"Hey, Roy." Not surprisingly, the man didn't even blink at Will's fake name. Never mind that Roy Rogers was an American legend. Most people saw and heard what they wanted—no more; no less.

Instead, he smiled, a red, wet-lipped smile that might have scared a lesser man than Will. "Buy me a drink?"

Under a few day's growth of beard, Will's new friend looked like he could stand to skip a few drinks.

"Sorry." Will shrugged and turned away, signaling his lack of interest and silently praying the man would move on. He was blocking Will's view.

Instead of leaving, the other man settled on the stool and lit a cigarette, adding to the cloud of smoke that hung thick as LA smog over the bar. Will narrowed his burning eyes and sighed, hoping like hell he wouldn't have to move. The only other good vantage point was across the bar, where a guy who looked big and intimidating enough to be one of Tommy "Lupo" Brown's thugs raised a beer to Will. He lowered his eyes, focusing on the glass of Guinness in front of him as the thump of the bass vibrated his eardrums. He wasn't exactly sure he wanted to sit next to a gay man who might actually stand a chance of beating him up.

Not that he *would* beat Will up, but if he tried, Will would have to shoot him. He really didn't need that sort of attention. And besides, hiding a body that big would take a lot of work.

He much preferred the precision and perfect execution of a well-thought-out job to a random kill. The unpredictable was destined to be messy and could land his ass in places he didn't want to be.

Like prison.

He'd had a few close calls. When you killed people for a living, that came with the territory. He brushed it off, trying to focus on the job at hand.

Derek Frost: Dark blond hair, 5'10", 180 lbs, brown eyes, pierced nipples (not that anyone but Will's current employer and Derek's lovers knew that), heavy drinker, and a predilection for gay bars even though he swears up and down he likes women better than men—but not by much.

For reasons that were of no interest to Will, Derek's business partner wanted him dead. Which explained why Will was currently sitting in a rundown gay bar in Phoenix, Arizona.

Derek was quite the social butterfly, though he had abysmal taste in bars—gay or otherwise.

Will's new friend finally gave up and left, and now Will had a bird's-eye view of Derek and Loverboy ensconced in a booth about ten feet away. Satisfied they weren't going anywhere for a while, he turned away before someone, anyone, noticed him staring at the couple. Once again he caught the eye of the man across the bar—the *big* one. Despite the dive status of the Oil Spout, Flirty seemed as out of place as Will felt. He shrugged, hoping the other man wouldn't take it as an invitation, and took a deep drink of his beer, letting the cool, dark brew slide across his tongue, savoring the thick, yeasty flavor while he turned his attention elsewhere. Like toward the two girly men there in the corner, having a bitch-fest complete with claws and pouty, scowling faces. Will waited to see if someone would throw a punch, rolling his eyes when all that happened was a slap.

So much for entertainment.

He took another small sip of his beer, not wanting his head clouded for the job in front of him. For the most part, Will could have passed any of these men on the street and they never would've known he'd spent the better part of his life as a professional hit man. Not that they probably cared one way or the other. He didn't bother sparing much brainpower on them either. Will cared about the job, his family, himself. And once upon a time, he'd cared about Tilly Acuna. Until Tilly had informed him he was as warm and passionate as a brick wall and suggested maybe he find a man to snuggle with from now on. He'd packed up his things and moved out, storing his stuff at his parents' place in Oklahoma City and taking this job. He'd thought that time and distance would help. They had, to a point.

Sadly, Tilly wasn't the first woman to point out his failings when it came to the fairer sex, and it wasn't just in the bedroom.

It was everything.

The flowers, the talking, the movies—how did women watch that shit? Anniversaries and her friends and his friends, and friends' weddings and babies and . . . in the end he'd decided maybe Tilly was onto something. Maybe he was gay. God knows he'd yet to find a woman he couldn't live without let alone a woman he could make happy.

And surely a relationship with a man would be . . . easier. *Much easier.* There'd be football and beer, tortilla chips and queso dip, belching, and no bitching about missed anniversaries or ditched dinner parties. Across the way, the two queens had devolved into a full-out slap-fest. The bartender opened the lift and stepped through, bat in hand, shouting at the top of his lungs. At that point, Will decided he wanted a real man. Then he accidentally caught the eye of the thug on the other side of the bar. He had a fresh beer. Now that was a man. A real man. Someone you could play softball and football with and . . . just then, Will's ass puckered.

He hadn't quite worked out the sex issue.

If given the choice, Will preferred killing from a distance. Times like these, he didn't always get his wish. Not that he was squeamish, but distance negated problems like fibers, witnesses, and DNA. Unfortunately, his quarry lived in a low-slung, one-story house smack in the middle of one of Scottsdale's nicer neighborhoods. That, combined with Derek's crazy work schedule, made a long-distance kill impossible. Too many unknowns: the neighbor out walking his dog late at night, the couple out for a midnight swim, a sick baby . . . all of them could bring Will attention he didn't need. And as close as he was to retirement, he wasn't about to risk spending the rest of his life in a ten-by-ten cell.

He slipped out of the bar shortly after Derek and Loverboy and followed them at a discreet distance in the black, '76 Monte Carlo he'd picked up in Flagstaff for a song. He'd chosen the older model car because it was heavy and fairly nondescript. If Derek ran true to form, and Will was counting on him to, he'd spend approximately ninety minutes with his new friend, then leave for home, stopping once to get cigarettes and a Dr. Pepper. Will followed them into the condo complex, cruising past as Derek and his companion stepped into a nondescript condo. He circled around to make sure Derek's car was still there, then pulled into a fast-food place across the road to eat—and kill some time.

As meticulous as he was, he could only plan things up to a certain point. The rest was left to the foibles of his fellow man, and if there was one thing he'd learned, man could fuck things up royally.

Luckily, tonight was not one of those nights. Eighty-seven minutes later, Derek's car pulled out onto the deserted streets. Will leisurely wadded up the burger he'd barely touched and threw it into the trash before starting the car. It roared to life as only a 405 could—with a predatory growl that would have scared off the fiercest jungle cats—and he backed out, his power steering squealing slightly as he turned hard on the wheel. He was in no hurry; he knew exactly where his quarry was going.

Home.

He followed at a leisurely pace, letting Derek get far enough ahead that he'd never dream he was being followed. After a while, the city lights disappeared and the darkness was occasionally punctuated by a porch light. Will slowed down as he came around a curve only ten minutes from Derek's home. The other man's elegant Cadillac was sitting on the side of the road thanks to an "untimely" flat tire. The car was an older model, pre-OnStar, and out here, cell-phone reception was spotty, thanks to the hills.

Derek was too drunk to change the tire, and yes, so drunk he shouldn't even have been driving in the first place. And he was *far* too drunk to do something as simple as call AAA when he could walk the quarter mile home.

Will rolled down the windows, slowing the car to a crawl and killing the lights. The late-night air was cool and damp as if weighted down by the quiet. He eased to a stop at the top of the hill, watching Derek get out of the car and slowly weave his way down the asphalt. Thanks to Will's slightly clammy hands, the steering wheel was a little slippery in his grip as he checked the rearview mirror for headlights. His oh-so-familiar case of nerves didn't come from a fear of getting caught so much as a fear of pesky human variables.

This was where weeks and sometimes months of planning and patience came in handy. Once he worked the execution of the job out in his head, Will didn't think too much about the actual person. He'd learned a long time ago it was better (read *easier*) if he kept things all nice and businesslike. His job wasn't just about killing. Any fool could kill. But a pro could make it look good, look like an accident, fate, or the luck of the draw, not murder. And Will *was* a pro.

Will's pulse picked up pace, his heart beating a rough tattoo in his chest as he glanced in the rearview one more time. Inky blackness greeted him.

And he had to get to Derek before he got much closer to the turnoff for his subdivision. The houses nearest the corner were quiet and dark as was everything for as far as Will could see. He sucked in a deep breath, blew it out, and pressed down on the gas, steadily accelerating, weaving down the two-lane road like a roller coaster picking up speed. The engine sang under the hood as he careened toward Derek, who didn't even realize he'd seen his last sunset.

And his last sunrise.

Will never slowed down as the car ate the road between them, never slowed down as the bumper kissed Derek, plowing him down, and the car rolled over him. He didn't slam on the brakes afterward, but slowed gradually so as to not alert anyone. The car finally rocked to a stop and he backed up, parking short of where Derek's body was.

Will snapped on some gloves, climbed out, and jogged to where the other man's body lay. His rubber-soled shoes were whisper-quiet on the asphalt. His quarry didn't move; the moonlight glimmered off the dark pool growing around his head. Careful to avoid the rapidly growing puddle of blood, Will reached down, checked for a pulse, then smiled in satisfaction when he found none. He stood for a moment longer, waiting to see if the man's chest would rise or fall, but it remained still.

Around him the night was so quiet not even a cricket dared to chirp.

Washing a car at two in the morning was out of the question, so Will parked (far, *far* away from the body) and wiped down the bumper and hood with some bleach water and paper towels. Crude maybe, but his cleanup job should, at the least, fool a cop in the dark. Back in the car, Will buckled up and pulled out a disposable cell phone. He sent a quick text message, slipped the SIM card out, and pulled back onto the highway. Once he felt safe enough, he tossed the card out the window, anxious to get to Tucson.

By tomorrow night he'd receive the last half of his fee, putting him that much closer to his retirement goal of ten million dollars (give or take, thanks to the costs associated with shuffling and hiding the money from Uncle Sam).

He was so tired that, by the time he hit the outskirts of Tucson, he could barely see straight, but his work was far from done. He turned off the highway and drove deep into the desert, heading for an old, abandoned gas station he'd found while doing recon. He'd left a second car there—a beat-up Ford Escort. A flashlight clutched between his teeth, Will once again went to work scrubbing minute traces of evidence off the Monte Carlo's grill, then he wiped down the inside of the car. He was counting on Mother Nature to obliterate his tire tracks as he headed toward Tucson in the Escort.

He parked the poor battered Ford workhorse on the top level of the parking garage attached to the hotel he'd checked into a week ago. He grabbed the black bag containing his favorite gun and a pair of gloves and crossed to the elevator just as the purple sky was growing streaked with sherbet orange.

Once Will dropped his bag in the Tahoe he'd left parked a few stories down, he headed for the hotel and a well-deserved rest.

He scrubbed at his face, his hands heavy with fatigue. A nice hot shower and couple hours of sleep and he'd be back on the road.

Will had just veered south onto the home stretch to El Paso when he spotted the ugly yellow van sitting on the side of the road ahead. At first he thought it was a trick of the sunlight, a figment of his fatigued brain, but as his Tahoe clicked off each tenth of a mile, he realized there was a woman standing next to the van, her skirt blowing in the breeze. He took his foot off the gas, tapping the brake and slowing to sixty.

He didn't trust anyone, not even a woman who *appeared* to be alone, but the manners his mom had instilled in him from a very early age made him pull off the road and back up. He jotted down the plate number, stowed the pen and paper under the arm rest, then shoved a Glock into the back of his pants.

Climbing out, he adjusted his shirt over the gun and assessed the situation. "Need some help?"

With her long skirt and the scarf wrapped around a mass of curly, dark brown hair, she looked like one of those Traveling Irish: modern-day gypsies. They didn't usually travel alone, so he took another long, hard look at the landscape, wondering if it was a trick. There was nothing but cactus and sand and shimmering heat in every direction for miles and miles.

"It's just overheated," she said.

"Want me to call a tow truck?" They were roughly thirty minutes outside of El Paso. Definitely close enough for one to come and pick her up (and he'd have done his good deed for the month).

"No." She had her hands tucked in the folds of her skirt, and her white blouse clung to her large breasts. She was pretty but sweaty and so hot her shoulders were bowed by the oppressive heat. She'd been out here a while.

"How about I take a look for you?" he offered, slowly moving closer.

"That's not necessary." The expression on her freckled face seemed wary and guarded as she shuffled from foot to foot. She backed up a bit, and he wondered what she was hiding. Just then a smallish mutt barked from the front seat. Despite his loud mouth, he looked and sounded about as ferocious as Odie from the Garfield cartoon.

"Shut up, Scamp!" She swiped a hand across her forehead and swayed on her feet, grabbing the van for support.

"How long have you been out here?"

"A while." She gave him a limp smile. "You're the first person to stop."

"I've got some water." He slowly moved toward the Tahoe. "Be right back." He got her a bottle of water from the cooler he kept in the back of the SUV, slammed the door shut, and headed toward her, only to find her on the ground.

Still clutching the water bottle, he rushed over, kneeling down on the asphalt, glad he'd worn jeans. He smoothed her hair away from her face, conscious of the constant barking of her dog and the bitter, pungent aroma of coolant seeping from the bottom of the van.

He carried her to the air-conditioned comfort of the Tahoe and laid her across the empty backseat. She was pale under her tan, and thick lashes caressed her red cheeks. He dabbed at her face and neck with condensation from the water bottle, breathing a sigh of relief as she finally came around.

"What's your name?" His tongue felt thick and clumsy in his mouth.

"Sabrina . . . Walker." She wet her lips with the tip of her pink tongue and struggled to sit up as the confusion that clouded her eyes dissipated. "What happened?"

"You fainted."

"Oh," she said softly. As if she'd just realized she was alone with him in the back of his Tahoe, miles from anywhere, she drew away and licked her lips. Her eyes were busy searching for a means of escape.

"It's okay." He pressed the open bottle into her hand, then slowly backed away, taking a spot on the edge of the seat so she'd have more room.

"You? What's your name?"

He stuck with what he knew, his brain distracted by her soft, puffy-looking lips. "Roy. Now, how about a ride?"

She sipped at her water, glancing around the SUV again. She finally nodded, slowly and with obvious reservations. "I need my stuff, and my dog."

※ ※ ※

Sabrina Walker fell somewhere between milk chocolate and café au lait. Her nose was small and puglike in a cute way, her eyes a hazel green rimmed with brown. Her lush lips formed a cupid's bow. He could thank his sister for that obscure bit of description. Sabrina's long dark curly hair was shot through with red and gold—the better to make things interesting. Some might call her plump, but no one would ever call her plain.

Her van was probably shot. He couldn't leave her sitting there on the side of the road to pass out again while waiting for help that might never come. Luckily, she hadn't argued; just grabbed her dog and purse.

He did the only thing he could. He'd loaded her and her damn dog up in his SUV. He figured he could find a garage in El Paso and buy her a meal while they waited on the tow.

"Why do you keep staring at me?" Her voice was husky, rough and unrefined like her.

He forced his attention back to the road. If he didn't stop staring, she'd jump out, moving vehicle or not. "Just wondering what you were doing out here in the middle of nowhere."

"Driving. You?"

Will laughed as much at her sarcasm as her smarts. She'd definitely been around the block a time or two. "Where you headed?"

"A Ren fair in San Antonio." The dog on her lap pawed at the console that separated them. He wasn't nearly as cute as she was, so Will frowned at him, hoping he'd stop before he marked up the leather.

"What the hell is a Ren fair?"

"You know, people dress up like knights and barmaids and drink mead and eat turkey legs. I tell fortunes."

"Fortunes." He snorted, thinking he told fortunes, too, but his were probably nowhere near as fun as hers.

"I'm actually pretty good."

"That's why you live in your van?" The words were out of his mouth before he could stop them, proving once again what an insensitive ass he was.

Surprisingly, she didn't rise to his unintentional bait. She just sighed, her fingers curling in her mutt's short hair as she glanced out the window. The Tahoe quickly carried them closer and closer to El Paso. In her lap, the dog whimpered briefly, raised his head, then settled back down as Sabrina stroked him. Her short, utilitarian fingers continued to gently knead as outside the SUV, the desert slowly, finally gave way to humanity.

All the while her silence dug at him, like a knife in his gut. "I'm sorry," he finally blurted out.

"Sorry for what?" She turned to look at him, her big greenish eyes curious.

"For what I said."

"Huh?" A slight frown puckered her brow. "What did you say?"

Here they went: the passive-aggressive, dog and pony show was on. Sorry was *never* enough. They always wanted more—blood, sweat, tears, your American Express card. Whatever... "My comment about living in your van. I'm sorry." *There! He'd said it.*

"Oh, sure." She shrugged in a way that made him want to hit her. Though as a rule he didn't hit women, with any other woman he would have gone three rounds by now. "No problem."

Of course there was a problem. There was always a problem.

And *problem* was spelled C-O-O-C-H-I-E. To get a little you had to give—*a lot*. Women were the scorekeepers, the referees, *and* the opponents, and men were expected to know all the rules; except they never let you see the rule book. Maybe he should just drop it for now.

"So what were *you* doing out here in the middle of nowhere?" she asked.

"I'm a salesman."

"Wow! Your company must love you." She patted the console, indicating the SUV's luxury package.

"I'm on vacation." Jesus, surely he could lie better than this! He had to get rid of her, and soon.

She was irritating him, getting under his skin with those big eyes and full lips. And those tits ... He turned the air conditioner on high and shifted in his seat, willing himself to not think about his cock—and her lips. Sabrina was off limits.

All women were.

He had to get rid of her and get back to Oklahoma and find a new place to live. Maybe a monastery. Did they even have monasteries in Oklahoma?

2

Roy was really starting to annoy me with that whole "stoic man" act. Soon as I found a garage to fix the van, I was out of here.

Gads, El Paso! It was so brown and taupe and dreary, the city bleeding into the surrounding landscape, letting the desert eat at it, suck it dry like a vampire. I shuddered, my fingers digging deeper into Scamp's fur.

"Can you"—I pointed to the fancy control panel on the dash—"turn the air down?" The arctic blast made me want to curl up in a ball underneath about a dozen blankets.

Grunting, he turned the knob and the air slowed to a nor'western.

It'd do.

I would have preferred the fresh air (even if it was hot as a jalapeño outside), but I was so grateful to have a ride I wasn't about to complain. My stomach rumbled, reminding me I hadn't had anything to eat since the vending machine donuts I'd grabbed early this morning. No wonder I'd passed out.

"You okay?"

"Just thinking about my poor van." And my poor savings.

"Maybe it's just a busted hose."

"Huh, more like a busted engine." I took another sip of my water, then let Scamp lick my wet fingers.

"You really think it's that bad?"

Swallowing the lump in my throat, I nodded. "There's a garage." I sat up a little straighter and Scamp wiggled in my lap, scratching at the door. He wanted out as badly as I did.

"Sure that's the one you want?"

"I don't care as long as they can fix a Chevy van." Geez, I wasn't exactly in a position to be picky. My stomach was already in knots over the impending expense, one I couldn't avoid.

"All right." He flicked on his blinker and took the exit. He turned into the little all-purpose gas station (the kind you don't see much of anymore) and jerked to a stop next to the pump. It was a concrete oasis with peeling paint and repair prices painted on the window.

"Will you watch Scamp while I see about a tow?" I scooted the puppy off my lap, holding him in place as I slid out. The Texas heat engulfed me, mercilessly driving away the chill brought on by the SUV's air conditioner. It was an almost instantaneous combination of sweat and scorched skin.

Roy stared at me as if he wanted to say no, as if he'd like to push the dog and me into the gas station's parking lot and take off in a squeal of tires, never looking back. "Sure."

The aviator sunglasses and the bland expression he wore made him unreadable, but something about him made me shiver as I closed the door. Scamp whimpered, his eyes mournful and anxious through the tinted glass. "I'll be right back," I mouthed, lightly tapping the glass.

Inside the building, a window unit was blowing full tilt, pouring damp, dirty-smelling air into every corner of the empty room. Three chairs were carelessly positioned against one wall, a white counter smudged with grease stains took up the other, and two metal stands held *Thrifty Nickels* and *Greensheets*. A rattling, gasping soda machine that looked almost as old as my van took up the remaining wall. The door to the garage opened with a squeal that made me cringe.

"Help you?"

"I broke down outside of town. Can you give me a tow?" *And please, God, can it not cost too much?* I sucked in my gut and gave him my best smile, hoping to win him over. "And take a look at my van."

Wiping his hands on a red rag, he looked me up and down, a slow grin crossing his sweaty, grease-encrusted face. He wasn't *bad* looking, but it had obviously been a while since he'd gotten intimate with Irish Spring and Mister Razor. He shrugged and glanced over my shoulder toward Roy's SUV, then stuffed the battered rag into the back pocket of his overalls. "I'm alone today, and pretty backed up."

Sighing, I forced myself to think of Scamp lying dead in the highway, and about how horrible I'd feel if I lost my only friend. Tears filled my eyes while my fingers knotted in my skirt. "I really . . ." I sniffed, raising my hands and waving them around helplessly.

"We close at six." He moved closer, close enough for me to see the avaricious gleam in his clear blue eyes and inhale the scent of his sweat mixed with grease. "I can take you out there then. Check out your van."

Check out my pussy was more like it. I bit my lip and raised my shoulder, getting ready to give him a nice healthy shrug, when the door jangled and Scamp barked.

"Your dog pissed in my car." Roy stood holding Scamp like he was some sort of diseased rodent. Scamp didn't look at all contrite. Or happy.

"I . . ." I glanced from Roy to Scamp to Garage Dude. "I'm really sorry." I reached for my puppy.

"What's wrong with your van?" the mechanic asked.

"It overheated," I said.

"I thought you said the engine was shot," Roy put in, taking away my chance to act dumb and helpless later when Garage Dude came to tell me that I'd probably blown the van's heads. They'd been on their last legs anyway, but I'd hoped the engine would hold out until after the fair in San Antonio.

"I *said* I hoped it wasn't."

"Can you fix her van?" Roy demanded, brushing at the front of his immaculate yellow polo shirt.

"I already told her it'd be after six before I could even go out there and get it."

"You staying here?" Roy asked, leveling his gaze on me.

"I'm . . . yeah." I nodded and sighed, glad I'd have Scamp for company. It was going to be a long day, in more ways than one.

"I'll take care of her." Garage Dude grinned, nodding in Roy's direction as if to possibly reassure him that I'd be fine.

I had a feeling the engine repairs were going to cost me bigtime.

Two hours later I stepped outside with Scamp on his makeshift leash. He'd started whining for another potty break. My back hurt from sitting for so long and I felt like I'd choke if I stayed in that stuffy little room. The late day sun, mixed with concrete, was almost unbearable; the pressure on my chest heavy as a ton of bricks. With the oddly hypnotic thrum of vehicles zooming past on the nearby highway for company, I led Scamp to a small patch of brittle, dry grass and waited while he did his business.

Garage Dude came wandering out, wiping his hands on that

rag while he looked me up and down again. He'd shrugged out of his coveralls, letting them fall to his waist. Forcing my lips into a smile, I motioned toward Scamp.

Don't judge. You can't survive out here on the road without having to occasionally do things considered *undesirable* by most.

He nodded, acknowledging he'd seen me, and more important, hadn't forgotten me, then reached up, revealing the sweat-stained armpit of his T-shirt as he pulled down the garage's door.

Apparently, the witching hour had come.

"Come on, Scamp." I tugged his leash, ready to head back inside for my purse when a shiny black van still dripping water from a recent washing pulled into the gas station.

I glanced at the grim-faced driver, then pushed the shop door open, ready to reclaim my place in Hell's waiting room, only to stop at the sound of my name. The door slipped from my fingers and huffed shut, pushing out a tiny bit of the dirty-tasting air. Scamp barked softly at first, then louder, tugging at his leash as if he'd just been found by his long-lost owner. As if he were actually happy to see the guy he'd peed on just a few short hours ago. Scamp tugged at the leash again, pulling me forward on reluctant feet.

"You're back."

Roy nodded slowly, a slight frown marring his forehead with horizontal lines. He tossed me a ring with two keys on it.

"What's this?" I held the keys up, then palmed them, the warm metal cutting into my hand, sharp and bittersweet as only hope can be.

"Keys."

I sighed, smothering the urge to scream, and just stared at him.

"Your stuff's in the back."

My eyes on his face, I crossed the hot concrete, then opened the side door. All my bedding, all my belongings were semi-neatly arranged in the van's carpeted interior. It smelled slightly like sweat and sand. Someone had made their home in this van before. Or done a lot of traveling in it. Swallowing the lump in my throat, I glanced at Roy, scared and slightly drunk on hope. In the past, she'd left me with a hell of a hangover. "Why?"

Scamp jumped to the foot rail, then clambered in, sniffing all around before deciding he must be home, since the twin mattress smelled like me. He walked in circles before settling down in a ball.

Lord, I envied him. I was so tired, but it'd be hours before I could sleep. "Why?" I asked again when Roy didn't answer. More important, how much was it going to cost me?

He shrugged, his shoulders rolling easily under his expensive shirt. "I assumed you couldn't afford to miss that . . . Ren fair."

I nodded slowly, wondering how I'd pay him back. Maybe he'd just decided that he wanted what I'd been willing to give the Garage Dude. "How?"

"Cash."

Cash always made things easier, but who the hell walked around with enough cash to buy a used van? I gave him a hard look but didn't have the balls to ask. It was that whole "gift horse" and "mouth" thing. "How much do I owe you?" All I had was $852 . . . and change. Not near enough to repay Roy for the van.

A few heartbeats later, he said, "A read. Do that card thing for me, and we'll call it even."

"*That's it?*"

He nodded tersely. There had to be a catch; nothing was free, few things were cheap, and desperate women were easy.

From the back side of the garage came the heavy rumble of a truck engine starting up.

I was a desperate woman. I glanced at the closed garage doors, then at Roy before slamming the van's side doors. He definitely qualified as the lesser of two evils. "Let's go."

Thanks to a green light we were back on the highway before the tow truck appeared. I was sure Garage Dude would be angry, being cheated out of an easy lay, out of as many easy lays as it would have taken to pay for the repairs on my van. "Where, uh, where should I take you?"

"Couple miles up. Get off when you see the Denny's." His voice was the texture of raw silk, soothing with a rough edge that didn't fit his smooth, nondescript exterior at all. It could melt butter.... Hell, it could melt me, and I'd happily give up a night, or five, to him in payment for the van.

Surely he wanted more than a *reading*.

The trip east through town was quiet. My nerves were taut, waiting for him to speak, to say something, to just come out and tell me he wanted to fuck me.

They *all* wanted to fuck me.

Not because I was pretty, or thin, or particularly exciting, but because they could. Or thought they could. Sometimes I didn't have to sleep with them to get what I wanted. Sometimes, I didn't have any choice. I figured it all balanced out in the end.

"*That* Denny's," he finally said, pointing.

"How'd you get this van? Seriously?"

"I found a guy who had a van to sell, and bought it."

"Did you make him a deal he couldn't refuse?" I quipped.

He snorted and his lips curved into a smile that softened his hard edges. It suited him. "The only deal I made him involved money."

"The van's not in my name."

"Yes, it is. Take this exit."

The van swayed slightly as I took the off ramp, then pulled into the parking lot next to his Tahoe. "You want that reading now?" I glanced at him again, then toward the back where my jumbled belongings were.

And how about a blow job while we're at it?

Smiling, he unhooked his seatbelt. "How about dinner first?"

"Sure." This day couldn't possibly get any weirder.

I cracked the windows and poured water into a dish for Scamp, who smiled appreciatively up at me. "Be right back, dude."

3

"So why'd you come back?" she asked once the waitress was on her way back to the kitchen with their orders. Sabrina crossed her arms on the table, her head cocked to the side, shoulders slumped slightly. She reminded him of that damn dog of hers, except he doubted Sabrina was the begging kind.

Why *had* he gone back? Will busied himself peeling the thin paper napkin from his flatware and laying it out. Stating the obvious would only embarrass her. She'd planned on sleeping with that disgusting, piece-of-shit mechanic to get her crappy-ass van fixed. And then it probably wouldn't have gotten her another thousand miles.

Make no mistake, he wasn't some damn soft-hearted killer with altruistic motives. He did what he did because he was good at it. Because it was all he knew, even if he was tired of it. And he wasn't out saving damsels in distress to salve his conscience or to make up for the lives he'd taken or because he needed to even the score with God. They had a gentleman's agreement.

So, even he didn't know why he'd bought the van. Not only

had he bought it, he'd followed the owner down the highway after spotting a FOR SALE sign in the van's window, and made him a great cash offer to get the deal done ASAP.

Even though it wasn't any more cold-hearted a transaction than him accepting money to kill Derek Frost, the thought of Sabrina sleeping with that slimy grease monkey while her stupid dog watched had left a bad taste in Will's mouth.

"Respect," he finally said, meeting her pretty hazel eyes. "I came back because I respect someone who does what it takes to get the job done."

She swallowed hard, nodding slightly. Her gaze shifted away from him and something like adoration filled her eyes as she stared at the van gleaming dark and shiny in the late afternoon sun. It was still old but at least ten or fifteen years newer than hers and well cared for. He didn't have to state the obvious. Sabrina was a survivor.

More important, she *knew* that he knew.

She nodded again, then muttered her thanks to the waitress who slipped a glass of Coke in front of her. "I can . . . do your reading after dinner. In the van."

And have sex.

The unspoken offer was tempting, but he didn't want her to think he was no better than that mechanic.

Not that he wasn't attracted to her. Sabrina was *gorgeous*, with an earthy sensuality that left his mouth dry and his cock hard, but pretty women were a dime a dozen and sex with Sabrina could only complicate matters in ways he didn't want to think about. He'd gotten enough of that with Tilly. "Why don't you just do it now?"

She blinked, her forehead furrowed in confusion. "Now?"

"Yeah, now. I've got to get on the road after dinner. My sister's waiting." *I'm not sleeping with you.*

Her lips twitched, then slowly curved into a smile.

"What?" Now he was the one confused.

She dug in her bag. "You don't look like the type to have a sister." Finally, she came up for air holding a handful of purple silk. With her other hand, she cleared the space between them, glancing around.

The restaurant was bursting with the early-bird-special crowd, but the corner they were in was fairly empty. She laid the square down, folding back sections of silk to reveal an oversized deck of cards with edges soft and worn from overuse. She shuffled repeatedly, silently, then finally fanned the cards out. "Think about what you want to know and then pick one card."

"Just one?" He'd only asked for the reading to appease her, figuring she wouldn't just take the van for *nothing*. He certainly didn't believe in her mumbo jumbo cards, but he chose, his hand hesitating, shifting down the deck and back again before finally settling on one card and handing it to her.

"The King of Wands represents you." Her eyebrow quivered slightly as she spoke; otherwise, her face was impassive. She didn't elaborate, and Will had no idea how he'd done. Not that he cared. Really.

This was for fun, right?

She laid out more cards, studied them, deeply immersed in her role as a prophet and giver of wisdom. Will hid his twitching lips behind his coffee cup, draining it and motioning to the waitress closing in on them for more.

"Thanks." He nodded, catching the surprised and skeptical look she shot Sabrina. Their eyes met, and he shrugged, as if to say, "What are you gonna do?"

Once the waitress was gone, Sabrina finally looked up at him, her gaze intense and probing. "The Knight of Wands here in the center"—she tapped the card—"signifies a trip or a move. Something unexpected. This one, here at the top, is your goal. But it's reversed, implying trickery. Something is standing in your way, preventing you from achieving whatever it is you want. Be alert, and decisive."

Will focused his attention on his coffee, biting back a snort at her theatrics.

"This one here at the bottom is the foundation your . . . desire is based on. The Ace of Wands implies a new beginning, like an inheritance, a child, marriage, an *adventure*. Something meaningful."

Here he smiled, thinking again of his impending retirement, the beach in Nevis, his happy bungalow, days of fishing and lazing in the sun, pulling his dinner from the ocean.

"This one here, at the bottom, she's the Priestess." She tapped the card thoughtfully, her lips pursed.

"What is it?" he asked, sounding more anxious than he would have liked.

"Well, it's someone you—an old influence, someone you've learned from."

Someone like his father who had been very vocal in his disapproval over Will's desire to quit. He'd been at it for almost ten years and his job didn't exactly come with a long shelf life.

"This one to the right is a new influence. The Emperor implies stagnation or a lack of progress. Slow movement. This one here, also at the bottom, is you and how you'll probably handle things." She stared at him, her gaze intense in a way that made him think he wasn't going to like what she said next.

"The Hermit signifies inner strength . . . or a loner incapable of interacting with others. There's a fear of discovery, of secrets and sometimes a failure to face facts."

She had no idea how close to the truth she was. He had secrets he could never tell a living soul. Ever. Secrets that could get him killed.

"This one here"—she tapped the next card up—"is your environment. Reversed, the Ten of Cups is about loss, family problems, strife." She shrugged almost apologetically.

He brushed it off, chalking it up to Tilly and his sex life.

She lovingly stroked another card, second from the top. "This is your hopes and fears. The Page of Wands is reversed, signifying an inability to make decisions."

Indecisive wasn't a word that could be used to describe him. He gave her a superior smile and leaned back so the waitress could slide his broiled chicken in front of him.

Sabrina ignored her and kept talking. "This card at the top is your outcome, but keep in mind, that can change based on your actions."

" 'K." He shrugged and forked up some broccoli, suddenly ravenous.

"The Chariot reversed implies defeat."

Before Will could form a reply, his cell phone rang. He checked the caller ID and flipped it open. "Yes, sir."

"I need you to check on your sister. She's down in Austin."

His sister wasn't really in Austin. Will had another job to do.

4

I took my job as a tarot card reader seriously and hated to be the bearer of bad news. Roy took it better than most. Okay, honestly, he seemed to totally dismiss my reading. Contrary to popular belief, readings aren't written in stone. They're only a foreshadowing of a possible outcome. Human nature, free will, can change things on a dime.

"Are you okay?" I asked, once he'd ended his call.

"Yeah, but I need to get going." He motioned to the waitress for the check, even though he'd barely touched his dinner.

"Thanks again. For everything." The dinner . . . the van . . . saving my ass. I didn't even want to think about where Roy had gotten the kind of cash needed to buy that van.

"Want a to-go box for that?" the waitress asked, motioning to my half-eaten burger.

"Yeah." I could share it with Scamp later on. Once she was gone, I turned my attention back to Roy. "Where are you going again?"

"Austin." He visibly paled. "My sister lives down there."

"Well, if you get bored, come check out the fair. It'll be fun."

I gave him a perky smile even though I doubted I'd ever see him again.

"Sure."

I reached in my purse and slipped a card out, sliding it across the table. "Call me. I'll buy you a turkey leg."

It was late, past seven when I climbed into the van and headed out of town on I-10, looking for a rest stop to bunk at for the night. Roy had even been kind enough to fill the gas tank. Unable to find anything that appealed to me or gave me good vibes, I kept driving until exhaustion finally forced me to pull off in Fort Stockton. In honor of the new van, I splurged on a cheap hotel room, crashing to beat the dead after a long *hot* shower.

The next morning I got up and spent some time organizing the van. I shook out the sheets, shifted the mattress until I was happy with its location by the back doors, and remade the bed. Then I turned my attention to organizing the milk crates. I'd learned early in my travels to minimize. There was no saving of random souvenirs from dates, boyfriends, or life events fondly remembered. Not even the hoarding of books to reread at my leisure. Only the most precious, prized possessions were kept. In this case, a few photos of my mother and myself on the porch of our house in Endicott. The neighboring houses were so close, it looked like the opening scene from *All in the Family*.

I tucked them back in their envelope and stowed it away for safekeeping. My one crate of books, most dog-eared and waterstained, was stashed behind the driver's-side seat. Will had neatly stacked the crates containing my miniscule wardrobe against one wall of the van, and I left them there for now. The four crates of journals were next. I quickly located and stowed three behind Scamp's seat, then turned to get the fourth, except . . . it was gone.

There were twenty-nine journals, one for approximately every six months since I'd turned sixteen. How much journaling I did depended on the type of year I'd had. Some years had been more . . . eventful than others, and some had left me more time to write.

Obviously.

I scrambled around the back of the van again, searching for the missing crate, only to come up empty-handed. Sick with dread, I ran inside to my hotel room, searching in there even though all I'd brought in with me the previous night was a duffel bag with the bare necessities. Scamp barked from the van's open doorways, anxiously wagging his tail.

"Shhhh!" I pressed a finger to my lips, afraid I'd get caught with the dog and have to pay extra for my room. My hands shook, my fingers turned clammy, and my stomach almost rejected the meager breakfast I'd fed it from the motel's vending machine. The fourth crate was nowhere to be seen.

As nauseated as the thought of driving the three hours back to El Paso made me, I grabbed my bag and closed the door. I had to have those journals.

Had to!

But God, the cost of gas to go back. I didn't even want to think about it. *Not* going back wasn't an option. I blew out a deep breath of resignation.

I threw my bag inside. "Get in your seat, Scamp."

I closed the doors, making sure they were secure, then climbed in, pointing the van west. The entire drive was a nightmare. The minutes and miles crept past as I fretted over someone finding my van, finding those journals, reading them, or worse, scattering them all over the highway. Frankly, they were worthless to anyone *but* me, nothing more than entertaining fodder or kindling for a fire, but they were *mine*. The thought of someone burning them made me press a little harder on the gas, even though I couldn't afford to get stopped by the police. If I went to jail, Scamp would go to the pound.

The van was right where I'd left it, fading yellow paint blending into the scenery. It looked even more pathetic than I remembered. I approached on light feet, the scalding asphalt slightly spongy. I glanced back at Scamp. He stood with his paws on the dash, watching me through the front window. The air was hot and dry, and the van's side door creaked open with a metallic squeal. Inside smelled like baby powder and grease . . . and old. Just *old*.

It didn't take long for my eyes to adjust to the dim light. And it didn't take long for me to see that the inside of the van was empty. Pathetically deserted.

Shit!

5

Will had driven as far as the Hampton Inn in Fort Stockton before pulling off for the night. While unloading the SUV he'd discovered a crate of Sabrina's journals. They would have been perfectly safe in his SUV all night, but curiosity had made him grab two of them and carry them upstairs to his room. He tossed them onto the dresser where they called to him while he showered and worked.

He'd memorized the job details his father had sent him. Acknowledgment wasn't necessary. He only needed to respond if he was unwilling to take the job. He was rarely unwilling and only drew a hard line at settling domestic disputes. Those were just messy from the word go, a prison sentence waiting to happen—unless you took out both parties, and obviously, that idea didn't go over well with the clients.

Once he was done, he'd stretched out on the cool confines of the queen-sized bed, the television turned to CNN and muted, and learned a lot about Sabrina's last year on the road. Fascinated, he'd stayed awake reading much longer than he should have.

Now here he was, sitting in a nearly empty restaurant, sipping coffee and waiting on his eggs and turkey bacon and reading about the life and times of Sabrina Walker: The Early Days. The pages were musty and filled with doodles of animal faces and tarot card figures, and elaborate girlish handwriting that slanted crisply to the right.

Note to self: stay the hell out of Alabama.
Jail sucks. Jail really sucks. I don't care what anyone says about "three hots and a cot," I'm never going back. I can see why my dad didn't want to go. Bastard.
Of course, dear old daddy wouldn't have had to blow the sheriff to get fed either.

The scalding hot sip of coffee Will had just taken turned sour in his mouth. He forced himself to swallow. This was definitely worse than the one he'd read last night. *That* one had detailed a pleasant spring and summer in Florida and Georgia working fairs with a guy named Wes. Apparently, when she'd turned west, Wes had disappeared with most of her money and things had gotten progressively uglier.

"Sir."

He looked up, blinking to clear the ugly visual of Sabrina sucking the dick of some red-faced man old enough to be her father, to find the waitress standing over him, plate in hand. He moved the journal, making room. Smiling, she set his eggs down and refilled his coffee cup, her eyes lingering on the book before she turned away.

His appetite ruined, he barely touched his breakfast, then tossed the journal into the back of the Tahoe with the rest. How the hell was he going to get them back to Sabrina? The phone number on the card she'd given him was disconnected and the PO box address listed probably didn't belong to her anymore. At least she'd told him where she was going.

He could have just thrown them out, and maybe he should have. But something stopped him. Probably the same unexplainable something that had made him buy her a van. Luckily, she'd never know he read them.

By suppertime Will was sitting in suffocating traffic just outside of San Antonio. He stopped for a newspaper and dinner at Chester's, searching for any information about the Ren fair. He finally had to resort to asking the waitress, who was happy to give him directions. Once he was done, he left a generous tip and took I-35 to the 1604 Loop West until he spotted the setup for the fairground in the distance. It was hard to miss. There were cars as far as the eye could see, and beyond that, what looked like a medieval village complete with flying banners had sprung up in the middle of nowhere.

"Shit," he muttered as he took the exit for FM 2789. He hadn't thought that finding Sabrina would be quite so difficult. He'd thought this would be a get-in, get-out deal. And after being on the road for so long, he wasn't in the best of moods.

He'd thought wrong.

Will parked, then took the long trek to the entrance, paid his fee, and stepped inside. Big-bosomed ladies in corsets and long skirts that dragged in the dirt crossed paths with families in jeans and T-shirts, munching on turkey legs and sausage on a stick, sharing funnel cakes covered in powdered sugar and fruit. Will's mouth watered at the sight; then he thought about how unsanitary and unhealthy eating one would probably be. And besides, his digestive system probably couldn't take it.

More people in medieval getup wandered past, the sound of lutes and harps mixing with the cacophony of screaming, excited, sweaty, sticky children. There were people *everywhere*. Sighing, Will headed for the information booth and bought a map.

He glanced down at the elaborate piece of paper in his hands. "How do I find a fortune-teller?" He felt stupid even asking.

The girl behind the counter sighed and rolled her eyes, her gum popping ninety-to-nothing. She swiped at her damp forehead and jabbed a finger at the map on the wall behind her. "The smaller spots for fortune-tellers are here, here, here, and here. And then some are located in tents." The look she gave him said, "That's all you get."

"Thanks." *For nothing.*

Outside, Will stopped long enough to grab a bottle of water. The array of smoked meats and sweets called him, tempting him, but he didn't have time. He had to find Sabrina, give her the journals, and get out of there before his head exploded.

Will passed more women—some attractive, many questionable—and men with swords. A dozen belly dancers went swirling by.

At one point, he had to step out of the way to let the "royal court" pass, and ended up inside the tent of an incense seller. The combination of smoke and a variety of scents left him sneezing by the time he stepped back outside into the fresh air. He blinked his stinging eyes and continued on, passing booths selling jewelry, crystals and rocks, fake swords, and low-tech games of chance, and there were lots and lots of kids.

Kids scared Will more than women did.

Finally, after nearly ninety minutes of walking the grounds, Will located Sabrina. She sat in a little tent, her lush lips curved into a smile, her damn dog curled up near her feet. A woman sat across from her and they were talking excitedly. The table between them was covered with a purple cloth and, even from a distance, Will could see the tarot cards spread out on the table.

Sabrina had covered the top of her head with a multi-colored scarf and the rest of it fell across her shoulders, the fringe mixing with a messy mass of curls. She laughed again, dimples flashing. Will sighed and sipped his water, resigning himself to waiting . . . until the dog started barking. Scamp leapt to his feet and stood at attention, his little tail waving back and forth like a flag. *Shit.*

Something like relief flashed across Sabrina's face, a smile teasing her lips. Then she turned her attention back to her client and the dog lay down at a soft order from her.

Finally, the other lady left after shaking Sabrina's hand.

Sabrina waved him over as if he were her next customer. "Have a seat."

Will glanced at the rickety folding stool. "I'll pass. Can you take a break?"

"Sure." She stood, her thick lavender skirts swishing around her ankles, a hopeful smile on her face. "You have my journals? Don't you? Please . . ."

"Yeah. I'm really sorry." Sorrier than she'd ever know. The visual of her and that sheriff filled his head, and he forced himself to mentally shake it off.

She studied him intently as if she couldn't quite figure out if he'd read them or not. He met her gaze head on, his own eyes never wavering. Finally, she sighed and grabbed the dog's leash. "Come on, Scamp."

The dog wound between her legs and Will's. "He likes you, you know."

"Let's get those journals." He didn't much care for dogs, especially ones that pissed in his Tahoe.

"Oh, that's right. Your sister's waiting."

He started slightly, then nodded his head. He shouldn't have been surprised that she remembered. She made her living paying attention.

It took them nearly twenty minutes in the sweltering late-afternoon heat to get back to his car, and by the time they did,

Will was wishing he'd broken down and gotten one of those turkey legs. His mouth fairly watered at the thought of biting into one, and damnit, he was starving.

Sabrina barely said two words to him the whole time. He knew what she was thinking, though. She was thinking about those journals. And whether he'd read them. Any normal human would have at least looked at them, but Will didn't want to acknowledge the fact that he had.

They closed the last few feet to his SUV. In less than thirty seconds they'd say good-bye.

Out here, so far from the fun and frivolity of the fair, the silence of the makeshift parking lot was broken only by the occasional passing car on the nearby two-lane road and their feet moving through the dry, trampled grass and loose dirt.

Will opened the back of the SUV and lifted out the crate of journals. "Can you carry these?"

"Of course." She reached for them just as her damn dog decided to take a piss right next to Will's foot. Mud and urine splattered his shoe. He glanced down at the mutt then up at Sabrina, whose cheeks turned pink. "He really does like you."

Will slammed the trunk and stepped over the dog, just as something bit the back of his hand. The pain had barely registered when Sabrina stumbled back a few steps, pale-faced and shaky, her eyes huge in her face, her whole body trembling.

Frowning, Will rubbed his stinging hand, only to have his fingers come away wet and red.

"Fuck!" He'd been shot. Cursing even more, he pressed his bleeding hand against his jeans to staunch the flow while shoving a swaying Sabrina between his car and the one next to it. Will dove down beside her and hurriedly patted her down, relieved when he found no blood or injuries. "You okay?"

She nodded, then said, "Your hand?" Her voice warbled and squeaked.

"I'm fine." His hand was slick with blood and burned, but he'd live. "Are you?" He peered around the back of the Tahoe just as the back side window shattered. A dusty black Monte Carlo sat on the farm road about fifty feet away. The passenger side window was down, and all he could see was the edge of a silencer.

"Roy?"

Glass rained down on them as one of the back windows exploded. Dread, cold and thick, filled him as the mutt darted over, settling on Sabrina's skirts. She curled up in a ball against the other car, her skirts covering her legs and hiding the dog from flying glass.

That Monte Carlo was the one he'd left parked in the old gas station outside of Tucson. He'd bet his life on it—and at this point, he pretty much was.

"Don't move." Will opened the driver's door and reached under his seat, pulling out his Glock. The other car was still there, engine thrumming while the driver patiently waited to take another shot.

"Roy?" Sabrina hissed. "What are you doing?"

"Stay here." At best he could get one or two shots off before the other car took off. Before someone came to investigate and *they* had to take off. He reached back inside, pulling out his duffle bag and throwing it next to Sabrina in case they had to make a run for it.

A shootout at the Ren fair corral was out of the question.

Will fired a couple well-placed shots inside the Monte Carlo's window, deciding more would attract the kind of attention he didn't want. Gun in hand, he crouched down, his back pressed against the SUV. Sabrina had deteriorated into a shaking bundle of brightly colored silks.

"Sabrina, calm down."

"He shot my journal." She lifted it out of the crate and showed him the bullet hole. "I was just standing there and—"

And Will had just signed her death warrant. She'd been seen with him. He checked through the broken window. The other car was definitely gone. He circled around the front, checked in both directions, and crossed to the wooden stake that marked the end of the parking lot. In the distance, he could see the car's taillights.

Reaching into his pocket, he pulled out his cell phone and punched in his brother's number. "I'm in trouble." It galled Will to no end to utter those words, let alone think them. But when forced to choose between Wynn and John (and their sister, who wasn't even an option), Will had decided the brother who *could* lie if necessary was definitely the better choice. "And Dad can't find out."

"Dad knows all and sees all, Will. You know that."

"Not this time."

"You in jail?" Wynn asked, his voice filled with disbelief.

Neither the Feds nor local police had ever connected a job to a Collier man, a fact Will's dad was incredibly proud of.

"No. Worse." He blew out a breath, surprised at how rattled he was as he glanced at Sabrina again. Will quickly filled him in, then dropped his voice, hoping Sabrina wouldn't hear him. "I'm not sure, but I think someone's put a contract out on me."

"I'll make some calls," Wynn said. "You stay safe and don't say a word of this to anyone."

They hung up, and Will turned to find Sabrina behind him, wide-eyed, pale, and, if he was right, angry.

6

"Why would someone put a *hit* out on you?" I stared at Roy, growing angrier with each passing second. My stomach quaked and my body trembled at the thought of how close I'd come to being shot. If I hadn't been holding my journals... I shuddered. I'd be lying on the ground bleeding.

I glanced at Roy's hand, then wished I hadn't. The oozing blood just brought it all back. God, I'd give anything to sit down. No telling how much longer my shaking knees would hold up. "*Why*, Roy?"

He stared at me, those chilly gray eyes unwavering. "It's difficult."

The sound of another car coming had him spinning around, his grip tightening on his gun as they passed on by. They never even looked in our direction. Just some farmer off running his weekend errands.

"And why do you have a gun? Are you a cop?" I took another hard look at him. "No, you're not a cop. So what are you?"

That cold, ugly piece of metal clutched in his hands was the last straw. My stomach rolled over and I hurled my tiny breakfast onto the bumper of his SUV. Even though a part of me knew it was my imagination and more than a few bad memories, the bitter, acrid smell of death and loss filled my nose and throat, choking me. I coughed and gagged, struggling to suck some of the hot, dry air into my lungs. I pushed away from Roy when he tried to help me. "Go to hell!"

"Sabrina..."

Pushing my hair out of my face, I glared up at him. "You make me sick."

He visibly flinched and paled, but the slight crack in his veneer quickly shored itself up, disappearing in the wag of a dog's tail. "We have to go."

I shook my head almost hard enough to make me dizzy. "I'm not going anywhere with you."

He grabbed me by the arm, hauling me to my feet. "If you don't come with me, you're a dead woman."

As much as I wanted to pray for someone, anyone, to come and rescue me, I knew it was useless. I'd have to rescue myself, just as I always did. How could I have so badly misjudged Roy? Not that I'd ever believed he was some random Good Samaritan or Robin Hood helping the poor and helpless, but I was normally a pretty decent judge of character. And I sure hadn't pegged him for the gun-toting type. "Are you FBI?" I asked, a part of me hoping he did undercover work. The rest of me was resigned to waiting for the truth.

"No, and my name's not Roy. It's Will, and we have to go. Where's your van?" He stalked past me, not waiting for a reply as he pulled another bag from the back seat.

"Then who are you?" I wasn't going anywhere until I got some answers.

"Later," he sighed. He slammed the door and slipped his sunglasses on.

"Now."

"We really don't have time for this."

"Make time." I crossed my rubbery arms over my chest, pleased when Scamp came to lean against my foot.

"I . . ." For the first time in our short acquaintance, he actually looked uncomfortable as he glanced around, "I, um, I'm a professional . . ."

"A professional *what*? You're not *the law*." I sniffed. "I can tell."

"Hit man." He said it so softly, his words took a minute to register.

I backed away, angling between the car parked next to Will's and the one nosed up to it. Had I heard him right? People didn't really . . . *really*, did they? Random acts of violence were one thing but . . . but cold . . . calculated . . . "I'm not going anywhere with you."

"You are if you want to live." He shoved his gun under his shirt, then picked up my crate of journals in his free hand.

"*No*, I'm *not*!"

"Sabrina." He sighed again, obviously losing patience. The parking lot appeared empty of humans and the gates a long way away, longer than I could ever hope to run and get away from Will/Roy. What passed for fair security was, for all intents and purposes, invisible. "They saw us together. If you don't come with me, you're dead. Now where's your van?"

"You kill people for a living." My stomach clenched from dry heaves as I wrestled my way between the two cars and started walking toward the entrance. I might not get far, but I'd do my best. I tugged at Scamp's leash, my feet moving as fast as I could make them. I didn't even realize I was crying until I tripped on the hem of my skirt and nearly fell.

From behind me came the sound of quick footsteps and Will cursing. I started to run, holding my skirts up, my Birkenstocks flapping against the sandy soil. Scamp barked, jumping and running beside me as if we were playing a game. I'd barely made it past half a dozen cars when Will caught my arm in a vise grip. A group in full costume, souvenir beer steins in hand, appeared from between two cars. I shot them a pleading look as Will spun me around and covered my mouth with his. His lips were hot and firm; an arm snaked around my waist.

I whimpered against his lips at the realization that he wasn't letting me go. No matter how much I argued or how far I tried to run.

I'd gotten myself into a hell of a mess this time.

Instead of a beagle I should have gotten a rottweiler. Sighing, I leaned against him, relaxing slightly, hoping he'd think I'd given in, but Will was no fool. I could feel the tears falling, my mouth thick with them as he finally let me up for air. He cradled my head against his chest, his good hand buried in my hair.

I sucked in a deep breath, inhaling the scent of sweat and man and . . . blood, then reared back and slapped him as hard as I could. "I hate you," I said, shaking the sting out of my hand.

"I'm sorry," he said gruffly. The sight of his bloody hand pressed to his cheek made me nauseated all over again.

"I'm scared." My voice shook.

"I'm sorry," he said again, his voice softer this time. "Truly. Sorry."

He dropped the crate and reached for me. I backed away, pulling my scarf from my hair. "Gimme your hand," I said, scowling.

While I wrapped up his injured hand, he rubbed my shoulder, his fingers occasionally pulling at my curls. Deliberate or accidental, I wasn't sure.

"Thank you," he said gruffly.

"Yeah, whatever." He'd never know how badly I wanted to bury my face in his chest and cry. Something I hadn't let anyone see me do since Ronnie died. "I should let you bleed to death."

"It's just a flesh wound."

Sucking in a deep breath, I forced myself to back away from the (questionable) safety of his arms. My little patch job would just have to do, though I wasn't even sure why I'd bothered. "I don't want to go with you . . . *Will*."

Sighing, he brushed some curls off my forehead. "I know. But if you don't and you die, I'd never forgive myself."

"Splitting up—"

"No." He shook his head for emphasis. "No splitting up. Whoever's after me isn't the type of person to play. They'll find you—"

"I'm not dumb. I know how to hide."

"And they know how to find you. It's their job, and they're good at it or they wouldn't have been sent after *me*."

Funny enough, I believed him.

"Well, that's what you get for killing people," I spat, hitting him in the stomach. He didn't budge. Just stared down at me with that grim, thin-lipped, "stoic man" expression. "Why should I pay for all the bad karma you've reaped?" I'd done that once, in another lifetime, and it had nearly killed me then. This time would be different. This time had to be different.

"If we split up, they'll find you and they'll use you to find me, and when you can't give them what they want, they'll kill you." He tucked my arm in his and turned me back toward the gates. "Together we stand a better chance."

"How long?"

"How long what?"

"How long do we have to stay together?"

"Until I find out who's after us and kill them."

A shudder ran through me, but this time I didn't throw up. There was nothing left.

7

Bags thrown over one shoulder, crate clutched between his fingers, Will draped his other arm over Sabrina's shoulders. Hopefully they looked like any other couple even though she was in costume and he wasn't. The last thing he needed was for her to run inside, hollering for the cops and blubbering about hired killers. Police involvement was bad, *very* bad. At the very least, it'd bring him attention he didn't need. But he had a feeling he'd convinced her to see things his way.

Neither of them spoke on the walk back to her spot. Even the dog stayed quiet.

"Do you have any idea how much money I'm going to lose?" she asked as she folded up the purple tablecloth.

"I'll make it up to you."

"Oh, I bet you're just *loaded*." She snatched the crate from him and pitched the cloth inside, followed by her cards. She quickly disassembled the table, her movements jerky, and shoved it at him. He'd barely gotten a grip on it when the crate landed in his arms. Clutching the little folding stools to her, Sabrina scowled at him, her eyes blazing.

"Let's go."

Will would have laughed at the way she'd "punished" him if the situation hadn't been so serious. Sabrina definitely knew how to make her unhappiness known. Sighing, he followed her through the crowd to the vendor parking lot, thinking of that turkey leg he'd never gotten.

"Gimme your keys."

"You're not driving my van." Shoulders stiff, she stalked around the front and climbed in, leaving him to ride shotgun. "You gave it to me. Remember?"

Except, when he got there, the seat was already taken. "Move, dog."

"His name is Scamp. Use it."

Will glanced at her over the top of his sunglasses, then back down at the dog. "Move, Scamp."

Instead of moving, Scamp sat, the doggie equivalent of "fuck you" on his face.

"Please," Sabrina said softly.

They really didn't have time for this. "Please." Scamp didn't budge. "Move, Scamp, please."

With one last nasty look, the dog turned, showing his ass to Will, and jumped down, disappearing into the back of the van.

"Lay down, Scamp," Sabrina cheerfully called, but the sarcasm wasn't lost on him.

The dog replied with a bark as he settled on Sabrina's mattress.

If Will knew one thing, he knew he'd have to find out who was after him as fast as possible. He didn't know how much of . . . Scamp . . . he could take.

Sabrina started the van, and abominably loud country music assaulted his ears. He reached over and lowered the volume. "Can you turn on the air?"

"No." She backed out.

"No?"

"No. Fresh air is better for you."

Fresh air that hovered right around 103 degrees. Groaning, he rolled his window down, sure he could persuade her to turn it on in the near future, when she finished punishing him. "Head for the nearest gas station."

"I've got a full tank," she said, pulling out onto the farm road.

Could she possibly argue with him any more? He scanned the countryside as far as he could see, but there wasn't a car in sight. "Head for the highway and find me a convenience store so I can get a disposable phone."

By the time he climbed out of the van ten minutes later, Will had a raging headache. "Want anything?"

"My life back would be nice."

"Besides that?"

"Beef jerky." She turned the music up and proceeded to sing along.

None of the cars looked like the one from the fairgrounds—thank God for small favors—but Will wouldn't be surprised if they were being watched. It's what he'd do. Of course, he wouldn't have missed his target in the first place.

Inside, the place was doing a brisk business, but he didn't waste any time. It wasn't like they'd shoot him here in front of all these people, but the faster he and Sabrina got back on the road, put some distance between them and here, the better. Will grabbed a couple packages of beef jerky, something for his headache, a six-pack of water and, after perusing the candy bars, some sugar-free gum. He never ate candy. He had never developed a taste for sweets, other than his mother's pie, but right then, a Snickers bar sounded like heaven to him. He also got the phone.

"Drive," he barked as he climbed into the van.

She stared at him, her gaze never wavering as she put the van in reverse. "You don't have to snap at me."

"You need to learn to move quicker." He set the bags between them and fished out the phone.

"I'd tell you to loosen up, but I'm afraid to ask what you do to relax."

"Drive." He snapped his seatbelt into place and threw her jerky onto the console between them. "Before someone makes it look like we've been carjacked and our bodies are found in a shallow ditch somewhere."

She drove, but Will regretted his words the minute they were out of his mouth. She didn't talk to him again until they hit New Braunfels almost an hour later. By then, Will had relaxed enough to tackle the distraction of another phone call. While the phone rang, he stuffed his trash in the bag and set it behind his seat. He wasn't willing to use his own phone and had even shut it off in case whoever was after him had decided to use it to track them.

"Hello," a female voice said.

"Let me talk to Wynn." From beside him, Sabrina snorted.

"Hang on." Julie sighed, and he heard the muffled sound of her shouting for his brother. Julie and Wynn had been married less than a year, and she still hadn't gotten past her disapproval over how the Collier men made their living. She would eventually, if she planned on staying married to his brother.

"This is Wynn," he said as Julie hung up.

"We're on the road."

Wynn snorted. "I'd ask who's got it in for you, but I'm sure the list is hellaciously long."

"Gee, thanks."

"Just saying, bro."

"Look, we're headed north on 35—"

"*We?*"

Will glanced at Sabrina. "It's a long story."

"Don't come here."

"I'm not dumb, Wynn." But he had no idea where to go and told his brother so. "I need a place to hole up."

"You want someplace in the middle of nowhere where you can see folks coming for miles, and run the risk of being trapped, or you want some place with lots of people where you never see the bullet coming?"

He should have gotten that Snickers *and* a soda. "You're not funny. *This* isn't funny."

"I'm not trying to be funny, Will. Now lighten the fuck up."

"Sorry," he said even though he wasn't. They needed to go to ground fast. "But I don't have a lot of options."

"Let me talk to Julie, and I'll call you back."

"Fine."

"Hey?"

"What?"

"Is she pretty?"

"Go to hell." He hung up, took his ibuprofen, and swallowed half a bottle of water as the rolling scenery raced by.

"You don't have a sister in Austin, do you?"

"No. She lives in Dallas."

"Is she a hit . . . woman?"

Will almost laughed. "No. She's a college student."

Danielle hated guns, hated how her brothers made a living. Will sighed, praying for his headache to let up, but he had a feeling it'd be a long time before it did.

"Will?"

"Hmmm?"

"Where are we going?"

"For now? North. Just north."

While Sabrina drove, he kept an eye in front of and behind

them. He sighed in relief when Wynn finally called back with directions to a lake cabin up by the Red River.

Will sat on the front porch, warped wood cutting into his ass, listening. For a car, for a rifle. For footsteps. He didn't expect them to come from inside the cabin, but a floorboard groaned, then another, then the door opened, scraping against the floor. Sabrina stepped outside, joining him on the porch.

The night was dark, and cool, thanks to a breeze off the water that also carried the sound of frogs croaking and rustled through the oak trees.

Earlier she'd said she hated him; now she sat leaning against him, arms wrapped around herself, the darkness and her hair hiding her face from him. The click of Scamp's nails announced his arrival. Instead of joining Sabrina, he jumped down the steps, sniffed around in the trampled yard a bit, then lifted his nose to the sky, smelling something.

Wetting his lips, Will tensed, his grip tightening on the gun cradled in his hand, but Scamp just resumed sniffing and walking. He disappeared around the side of the house.

Will couldn't blame Sabrina, but ever since he'd met her, his life had spiraled out of control and that didn't sit well with him. Here he was, on the run with this strange, beautiful little vagabond. It scared him to even admit to himself how beautiful she was. Now was not the time for physical complications. Matter of fact, it was the worst time. They had enough to deal with.

They sat silently for a while listening to the wind scuttle through the trees, watching the clouds race across the moon to occasionally darken the yard. The heat of her body warmed him as the night deepened.

"You should get some sleep," he finally said. There was no

telling what tomorrow would bring, or when whoever was hunting them would finally find them.

"I still hate you." Her voice was soft, and there was no oomph behind her words.

"I know." He sighed, but made no move to comfort her. His body felt like he was wearing a lead suit that prevented him from moving.

She curled up smaller, resting her head on her knees.

"There's a bed inside," he said, giving her another verbal nudge. "You should use it."

She sat up, flinging her hair over her shoulder and frowning at him. "Are you always such a coldhearted bastard?"

No reply was necessary; the one he would have given would probably have gotten him slapped anyway.

"I'm not exactly in the mood for sleep, okay?" she said, her voice warbling with fatigue and emotion. "You don't even care what you've done. What you've done to me and Scamp." She motioned to the dog, who'd found a nice spot in the yard to lie in. Unlike her, Scamp didn't seem terribly concerned with their new circumstances.

Will heard her words, felt her pain, but finally realized he didn't know how to respond. Women confounded him. Even his own mother, whom he loved more than anything, had left him scratching his head more times than he could count.

"You can ignore me all you want, but you can't shut me up. I am *not* going to die because of your bad karma." She took a deep breath and shouted at the top of her lungs, "Do you hear me?"

Will winced as her words echoed off the hills around them. "Like you have a lot to live for?" he snapped back, his patience worn thin.

She lurched to her feet and dusted off her backside. "You're as warm as a side of beef in a meat locker." She went back inside the cabin, slamming the door behind her.

He sighed again, hanging his head. Give him a gun, a job, and a time frame, and he knew exactly what to do. Give him a woman, and he was lost as . . . well, as lost could get.

Scamp's tag jingled as he got up. He stopped briefly to lick Will's fingers, then headed for the door. He scratched twice and a few seconds later, Sabrina let him in, slamming the door again.

Shutting Will out.

He should go inside and talk to her, apologize, but words failed him and so did his legs. What good would apologizing do anyway? It wasn't as if he'd missed a birthday or an anniversary. He'd put her life in jeopardy. Will deserved her anger. He just wished he knew how to comfort her.

He came awake in an instant, his heart pounding as he lurched to his feet and swung his gun to the left, his gritty eyes trained on the corner of the house. The sound of his brother Wynn telling him to relax had him sagging against the porch post, the hand holding the gun falling to his side. Wynn was taller than him by about four inches and as solid as that chilly side of beef Sabrina had mentioned. Marriage hadn't made him lazy, but he was definitely eating better.

"Morning."

Wynn returned his greeting, the corners of his eyes crinkling. "You look like hell."

"Gee, thanks." Will rubbed at his face, his palm scraping against a day's growth of beard. He felt like hell, too. And he didn't think his ass would ever recover from his long night on the porch. "What do you know?"

He led Wynn inside the cabin. It wasn't much, just a room with a tiny kitchen, a double bed, a sofa, some lamps, and a television that according to his sister-in-law got three channels—on a clear day. If the wind blew right.

"You need to do something about her," Wynn murmured, motioning to where Sabrina lay. Her face was hidden by a mass of hair, and she barely moved. At her feet, Scamp looked up, ears at attention. Once he'd decided they were no threat, he curled up again.

Will crossed to the battered coffeemaker and turned it on. "I know." Boy, did he know. He'd spent most of last night trying to figure out what to do with her. He'd dragged her into this and he had to get her out.

He had to figure out how to get them both out.

8

"You can't hide out here forever," the other man said.

"Here" was some remote lake in far North Texas. We'd driven, and driven, and *driven*, heading west once we'd gotten to Gainesville and losing ourselves in ranch country.

"I know." That was Will.

I slowly pulled back the covers and peeked at them both, startled to see how much the other man looked like Will, except taller. And cuter. As in puppy-dog cute. While Will was unassuming, boy-next-door-all-grown-up good-looking. They were obviously related and both of them would get better with age. But right now Will looked as tired as he sounded, and he hadn't come in all night. I'd stayed awake as long as I could, worried about where he'd sleep. I should have known better.

"And you can't go anywhere near Mom and Dad."

"No shit. You've got to find out who put a hit out on me. Before Dad gets wind of this."

"And *why*."

"They had the Monte Carlo—from Phoenix."

They moved outside, leaving me alone and wondering what

they were planning. And I didn't even want to know what had happened in Phoenix. I grabbed some clean clothes and headed for the bathroom. Despite plenty of sleep, I still felt tired and I couldn't shake the painful knot between my shoulder blades.

Back out in the kitchen, I noticed our guest had apparently brought food. I poured myself a cup of coffee and rifled through the supplies in a box, then made a peanut butter and jelly sandwich. I was thoughtfully nibbling at the crust when Will reentered the cabin, alone.

"You're up."

"Where's your friend?" I took another bite of my breakfast, nearly choking on the thick peanut butter and the fear clogging my throat. Hot coffee helped dissolve the peanut butter but not the lump.

"He left." He collapsed in a seat across from me, his gray eyes darkened to charcoal. A frown furrowed his eyebrows.

"Why couldn't I have gone with him?"

"Because I need to keep my family out of this."

"So it's okay to put *my* life in danger." I left my words dangling there between us.

"That's not what I meant, Sabrina." He blew out a heavy breath and his shoulders sagged. His head sank into his bandaged hand.

"How's your hand?"

"Fine."

"I can make you a sandwich." It was a lame peace offering.

He shook his head and looked up long enough to give me a brief smile.

"What's the plan?"

"We'll stay here for a few days."

Because you have no idea what the plan is. I frowned at him, letting him know that *I* knew he had no plan of action. I sat at the table, the hardwood chair biting into my ass, and finished my breakfast.

"Hopefully my brother can find out something, and fast."

In another world, under different circumstances, I wondered if Will and I would have met. What would have happened? If he would have asked me out, what would dinner and a movie have been like? Considering I liked Indie films and he probably liked action flicks, not so good. Then again, someone like him wouldn't have asked me out in the first place.

Will was a damn fine specimen, if you could get past the whole "killing people for a living" thing. Even with the shadows under his eyes and his normally pristine clothes now wrinkled and smudged with dust and dirt.

But he was still handsome in a way that made *not* staring difficult.

"Are we safe here?" I finally asked.

"Yeah. For now." He nodded, then stared at me slow and steady as if he could silently assure me things would be fine.

I nodded and nibbled at my sandwich until it was gone. "Is anyone going to . . . miss you?" Like a wife or a girlfriend . . . or boyfriend, though Will didn't really put off any "gay man" vibes.

"Just my family."

How ironic that a hired killer had a family and I didn't. "You were supposed to go on another job? Weren't you?"

Nodding, he lurched to his feet. "I'm gonna take a nap. Don't go outside."

Don't go outside, my ass.

I watched as Will dislodged Scamp from the bed and stretched out. The dog came over and started munching on the kibble I'd brought in from the van. I sat silently, waiting until Will's soft snores filled the cabin, then glanced down at my dog. "Come on."

* * *

I quietly slipped out the door, never looking back as I made the walk to the end of the driveway where I debated which way to go. It was a beautiful early summer day, the thick trees that surrounded the cabin still lush and green. Somewhere nearby a boat engine roared. The air was warm and slightly damp.

A stiff breeze stirred the reddish soil that made up the road and rocked the rickety mailbox back and forth on its rotten post. I glanced down at Scamp, who was waiting for me to make a decision. Just like he'd waited on me so many times in the past. Much like my poor, not-so-sainted mother, I'd made a slew of wrong turns. Unlike her, I knew how to turn my ass around and get the hell out of Dodge. Until now. Now it looked like I'd gotten myself into a hell of a mess. That didn't stop me from worrying that Will was right: if I ran, they'd find me.

Scamp trotted a few paces away, drawing my attention back to the here and now. I finally decided to go right; my flip-flops quickly grew gritty from the road, my feet covered with a thin layer of dust. Around me, the world seemed to have stopped. My fingers itched for my journal. I wished I could empty my brain of all its clutter, but I had a feeling that Will wouldn't appreciate me cataloging my adventures in Hit Man Land.

I passed a few empty double-wides and kept going until I hit a dead end. I stepped onto the porch of a rickety white house that actually looked worse than the cabin we were in. Despite the boat I'd heard earlier, everything was pristine and quiet, the lake like rippling glass.

I didn't just want to live, I feared death. The ugliness and the violence of seeing it firsthand had left an indelible mark on me. I sat for a while, letting myself get lost in the day and letting Mother Nature soothe me until Scamp's scurrying around and the movement of the sun got me moving again. As I headed back toward the cabin, it crossed my mind that I should probably be afraid, that I should leave Will here and let fate deal with him, but in some strange way, I felt like I owed it to him to stick around after he'd saved my ass twice in El Paso.

He was sitting on the porch angrily masticating a sandwich when I got back. "I thought I told you not to go anywhere."
"You did." I climbed the steps and walked past him, silently reminding myself once again that it was my van (even if he had bought it—and swiped the keys once we'd arrived here) . . . and I could leave any time I wanted.
"Do you have a hearing problem?" He scowled up at me. If anything, he looked worse than before he'd taken a nap.
"No, but I do have an ordering problem. You're not the boss of me."

9

Will was in deep shit.

Real deep shit.

When he couldn't find Sabrina, he'd dashed outside. At the sight of the van still parked next to the cabin, anger had replaced his fear. He'd immediately headed back inside and rehid the keys. Then he'd waited and waited for Sabrina to return. He'd moved from his spot on the porch just long enough to fix some lunch, then settled back on the steps where he'd spent most of the previous night. He'd figured—and rightly so, if her dusty feet were anything to judge by—that she'd gone out for some fresh air.

Figures she couldn't be bothered to listen.

But what really got to him wasn't the sense of relief he'd felt when he'd spotted her at the top of the drive, but the way he'd found himself watching her. The sun made her hair look all fiery; her curls and breasts bounced, and hips had rolled and swayed as she'd closed the distance between them. He'd nearly choked on his food. His blood had warmed, thickened, pooling in the most uncomfortable of places. He would have killed for a cold shower, figuratively speaking. He'd *never* kill for something so mundane.

Sabrina Walker was a beautiful woman. Not that he'd never noticed before. But somehow, in the last twenty-four hours, things had changed.

When she sassed him and said he wasn't the boss of her, he'd almost laughed.

"You've got forty-eight hours to figure something out and then I'm leaving."

Her words had the same affect on him as the shower he'd wished for only moments earlier. "You can't leave."

"I can, and I am."

"If you leave, they'll find you." And they'd use her to get to him. He couldn't allow that to happen.

"No, they won't." She shoved open the cabin door.

"Sabrina."

"What?" she asked, refusing to look at him.

He inhaled, wishing he hadn't as he caught a whiff of her: female sweat, her sex, and whatever it was that made Sabrina smell like . . . Sabrina. He shoved the thought of investigating further away. "You can only run for so long."

"And then what happens?"

"They catch you." The end result of her being caught hung between them, thick, heavy, and unspoken.

"I can run for as long as I have to." She stepped inside the cabin, but Will would have the final word in this round.

"God knows you're good at it."

She slammed the door, and he retrieved the gun he'd tucked under his leg at her appearance.

Will knew human nature.

Sabrina knew how to run.

But she couldn't run forever. He knew better than anyone

that, at some point, they'd have to turn and fight, no matter how badly he wanted to protect her. Failure was *not* an option.

He left Sabrina alone, the sound of running water keeping him outside, away from her and her shower, his head filled with images of her naked, wet, and warm, laughing up at him, those odd green eyes flashing and teasing. He could almost feel her slippery skin under his fingers.

Groaning, he lurched to his feet and took a walk of his own, wondering how he was going to survive the next few days stuck in the middle of nowhere with Sabrina.

While she was gone, his curiosity and more than a touch of anger had driven him to grab another journal from the van. He glanced at the cabin, pulled it from the back of his pants and tucked it under his arm, finally settling on the porch of a rickety house at the end of the road. Sabrina had been here, he could tell by the tiny paw prints Scamp had left behind in the sandy soil. If anything, the writing in this one was curlier, more girlish, and the reason was quickly apparent. It dated back a few years before the other one, from when Sabrina had still lived at home.

My mom is so dumb. How dumb is she, Sabrina? She's so dumb, she married the first jackass who asked her. I will never be dumb.
I will never be dumb about men.
I will never ever be dumb ever!

What had Sabrina wanted, planned? How had she thought her life would turn out? Apparently, she hadn't been much of a journaler then. The next entry was dated six months later.

My mom is so dumb? How dumb is she, Sabrina? She's so dumb, she's pregnant. Hell, even I'm on the pill. Not that she knows it, which goes to show how super-dumb she is. She's not even happy. Neither is Walt. I wish she'd never married him. Mom said she thought everything would be fine. Marrying Walt would fix everything. When I asked her what everything, she didn't have an answer for me. Adults are dumb.

The next entry was dated three weeks later—and water stained.

My mom is so dumb. How dumb is she, Bree? She's so dumb, she's dead. Just dead.
No way in hell am I staying here with Walt either.

It was dated almost ten years ago.

Will knew in the nauseatingly twisted depths of his stomach that those were tearstains not watermarks. Though her journal *had* gotten wet at one time. The pages were stiff, some stuck together, and water had smeared some of the ink on other pages. There were no clues as to how Sabrina's mom had died, but it obviously hadn't been pretty. From what he could gather, she'd taken Scamp (Walt's dog) and hitchhiked to Florida.

Back at the cabin, Will quietly replaced the journal, resisting the urge to grab another. If she found out he'd been reading them, she'd have his head for dinner. He smiled slightly at the thought, then forced himself to wipe the grin from his face as he stepped into the cabin. The fading sun had made the room almost unbearably warm, and he left the door open to help cool things off.

"There's not much for dinner."

The table was set nice, and she'd fried some hamburger patties and made macaroni and cheese. "It's fine."

"Go wash up."

He didn't just feel like hell; he looked like it, too. She didn't have to say it. He stepped into the bathroom, promising himself a shower after dinner and wondering how he'd get through the long evening ahead.

Turns out, he didn't have to worry. Sabrina apparently had no interest in speaking with him beyond what she could get away with. Even Scamp ignored him.

Will ate quickly to ensure his body had the fuel it needed. He wished Wynn would call him with information. Will hated sitting here, like a lame duck waiting for an invisible bullet to pierce his skull and take him down.

He did the dishes without being asked, his mind turning over the who, what, when, where, and how of it all.

Who wanted him dead?

What had he done to warrant a hit? Had he killed the wrong person? Botched a job? What had triggered it all? And how had they found the Monte Carlo?

When had he crossed the line from hunter to hunted? And how had he not known?

Where would he die? He'd never imagined it would be like this.

And most important of all, why?

Why had someone taken a hit out on him? Why did they want him dead?

If he really thought about it, dying by hired killer was fitting in some twisted way. Maybe even better than he deserved. But he was the oldest, the strongest, the fastest Collier. He'd been blessed with the best instincts of all his brothers.

And, if he could help it, he wouldn't die today, or tomorrow or anytime soon.

10

Wondering what had Will so deep in thought, I reached over and flicked off the kitchen tap. On second thought, it was pretty obvious. He was thinking about *us*, here, trapped like fish in a barrel.

He looked down at me, his eyes hotter, more intense than I'd ever seen them. "We're not going to die."

Sorry, but I wasn't convinced. And, as a rule, life-altering events didn't come with a money-back guarantee. "Everyone dies."

He nodded in acknowledgment and said, "Maybe so, but not us. Not anytime soon."

"You don't know that," I insisted. Surely he wasn't that naive.

"You are the most confounded fucking woman I've ever met in my life."

I turned away and bit my lip, unsure of what left me more tickled: The use of *confounded* or the fact he'd said *fuck*. I was too tickled to even get mad over being insulted. "I am what I am, Will."

"I know." He said it in a way that made me stare. Almost smug. As if he knew me so well when, in fact, he didn't know me at all. He wiped his hands on a dishtowel, then proceeded to wipe down the counters. Maybe it made him feel better to clean. Maybe cleaning was second nature for him, seeing as how he made a living cleaning—in a way. I guess, in his business, you had to be tidy.

Will folded the towel with deliberate, precise movements. He had beautiful hands, long fingers, trim, tidy businesslike hands. I guess hands were important in his line of work, too. Will had amazing hands, the kind that made me wish I was a palmist instead of a card reader, just so I could touch them.

The night stretched out in front of us, with no television beyond a fuzzy rerun of something I couldn't name, no radio, nothing. As repulsed as I was by how Will made a living, there was a part of me that wanted to know more. To understand him. Chalk it up to research, but maybe, if I understood him, I could figure out my attraction to him. "How many people have you killed?"

He smoothed the dishtowel out as the longest five seconds of my life ticked by. Finally, his head slowly swiveled so he could look at me through narrowed eyes. "*What?*"

I swallowed the lump in my throat and repeated myself through lips numb with fear. "How many people have you killed?"

His eyes were chilly-cold, scary-cold: the color of stainless steel. "A lot."

I should shut up now. I really should but I couldn't seem to stop despite his obvious anger. I struggled to keep still, keep breathing. "Up close?"

"I think there are some cards in the nightstand drawer. Why don't you go get them?"

"Answer the question."

"Go get the cards," he countered.

"Answer the question."

"A few times. Now—" He gave me a pointed look, one eyebrow arched. It said, if I knew what was good for me, I'd shut the fuck up . . . like ten seconds ago.

I shut up and went to get the cards, tossing the rubber-banded pack onto the table. "How do you usually kill people?"

"With a gun." He straddled a chair, ripped off the rubber band, and started to expertly shuffle the cards. "You play poker?"

"No." I moved closer, wanting to ask him more even though I sensed he just wanted me to shut the hell up. "Why?" I asked, taking a seat.

"Why what?" He started dealing out the cards, one stack for each of us.

"Why do you kill people?" I scooped up my cards, organizing them by suit and color, even though I had no idea what we were playing.

"Why do you read tarot cards?"

"It's my job."

"Exactly."

I watched him organize his own cards, once again drawn in by his hands. They were lovely, sensual, and capable of so much more than his chosen occupation. I wondered what it might be like to let him touch me, then pushed the thought out of my head, refusing to think about it.

"The game is Go Fish."

"Go *Fish*?"

"You said you didn't know how to play poker. So the game is Go Fish. You do know how to play?"

Of course. Everyone knew Go Fish. I'd played it with my mom lots of times and told him so.

"So you and your mom played. Do you have any nines?"

"Go fish." He pulled a couple cards from the stack then set down a pair of nines.

"Where's your mom now?"

I studied him over my cards, but his face was impassive. "Dead. Do you have any tens?"

"It's still my turn." He eyed me briefly; his expression gave nothing away. "How did she die?"

"Someone shot her." I stacked my cards in my hand, ready to take another walk if he didn't stop. "Planning on going anytime soon?" I didn't want to talk about my mother. She was none of his business. Maybe turnabout was fair play, but that didn't mean I had to like it. "What about *your* mom?"

He glanced at me really quick, then back down at his cards. "She's alive."

My knee started to jiggle underneath the table. "How does she feel—"

"Do you have any twos?"

I handed over a two and finished my sentence. "About what you do for a living?"

"I never asked her." He fiddled with his cards a bit, rearranging them. I found that hard to believe. Not that Will struck me as a mama's boy, but how could his mother not have expressed an opinion over his chosen occupation?

"Your dad?"

"Do you have any sixes?"

"No."

"Go fish." Will looked up at me, something about his expression making me think this was a life-and-death game, something more serious.

I frowned back at him. "Huh?"

"You're supposed to say 'Go Fish.' "

My word! "Go fish."

He drew a card, apparently not getting what he wanted.

"You're funny."

He grunted.

"You kill people for a living but you follow the rules for Go Fish to the letter. That's funny, ya know? Real ironic."

"Why are you so hung up on what I do for a living?"

Cheeks flushed, he slammed his cards down on the table and pushed his chair onto its back legs.

I set my own cards in a neat stack and let my shoulders slump from fatigue. "I've never met anyone like you."

"It's my job," he ground out roughly. "It's not who I am."

"Could have fooled me."

"What the hell does that mean?"

"What do you do for fun, besides play Go Fish?"

"I fish."

Unable to help myself, I laughed while Will lurched to his feet and stormed out, slamming the door behind him. I felt bad, sort of . . . a little.

Okay, not much, but you have to admit that it was funny. In a twisted sort of way. I hadn't meant to hurt his feelings.

Sighing, I gathered the cards together and put them back in the nightstand. Scamp scratched at the door and I let him out, watching as he nudged Will's elbow. Will lifted his arm, letting the dog crawl onto his lap. I could feel myself frowning, and a hot, jealous ache sunk its claws into my chest.

For the first time ever, I found myself wondering about my dog's ability to judge people. He'd always been really good at it. Better than me even. Then again, we didn't usually spend a lot of time with other people. Even those times we lived on-site at a Ren fair for weeks at a time, I tended to keep to myself. As much as I moved around, it was just easier.

I suppose, apart from me, Scamp hadn't spent a lot of time around other people, but still, seeing him cuddled up in Will's lap, Will's fingers digging in his short fur, made my heart hurt. Scamp was *my* dog, and I'd never had to share him with anyone before. Not even Walt.

From the minute Walt and Scamp had moved in with Mom and me, Scamp had attached himself to me, as if he'd sensed we were destined to be together. As if *he* could tell the future.

* * *

Will didn't turn around. I wasn't ready to apologize, not with Scamp's abdication so painfully fresh. I gingerly closed the door and stretched out on the bed, watching what was left of the sun travel across the ceiling until the cabin was almost completely dark. I dozed, slipping into that dark place that gave me murky restless dreams, until something pierced my sleep. I laid there blinking against the dim assault of the kitchen light, heart pounding as the sound of gunfire prickled my ears and finally registered in my brain.

The cabin was empty. I lunged upright and dashed outside. More gunfire filled the velvety dark night as Will grabbed me, yanking me behind the porch.

"I need to see where it's coming from." "It" needed no explanation, and "stay here" didn't have to be said.

I would have stayed put, too, if Scamp hadn't followed Will.

"Scamp," I hissed into the gloom, struggling to adjust my eyes. All I could do was track the jingle of his collar. "Scamp," I called, louder, repeatedly, but he was gone. I slipped off the porch and cut through the trees after him. After nearly twisting my ankle as I stepped into a slightly washed-out area, I grabbed onto a tree and caught my breath. Fear that someone might shoot Scamp in their quest to kill Will kept my feet moving.

When I broke through the trees, I skidded to a halt, using Will's back as a wall to stop myself.

I sagged against him, almost giddy with relief as a group of men took turns aiming at a row of beer cans—not all of them empty—and laughingly fired an assortment of firearms. "Well, I guess that answers that," I muttered.

"What are you doing here?" Will didn't bother turning around, just tossed the words over his shoulder.

"I was worried about you." We both knew that was a lie, but

he didn't bother correcting me. He didn't need anyone worrying about him.

The yard was lit by a bonfire and filled with men and women, most of them dressed casually. From the lake came the distinct sound of a woman's screams, splashes, and laughter. How we'd missed their arrival, I don't know.

"Go back." Will turned and none-too-gently shoved me toward the trees, when a woman's voice stopped us.

"Ya'll friends of Lisa and Kevin's?"

Will shoved me toward the trees again. "No."

"Stayin' 'round here?"

"Yeah—"

"We heard the shots," I added, maneuvering around Will to check her out. She was young, fit, and tanned, with a perky smile on her expressive face. Her hair was caught up in a ponytail; she wore cutoffs, flip-flops, and a bikini top, and she sure didn't look old enough to be holding that beer in her hand. But who was I to say?

"That was just some of the guys having fun."

Will nodded, though I wasn't sure he was totally convinced, and draped a protective arm around my waist. "We need to get going."

"Ya'll on your honeymoon or something?" She gave us a conspiratorial smile. Her left hand was bare, but I'd bet beers to bullets she was well-versed in what happened on a honeymoon.

"Yes." He dragged me backward a few steps on feet numb from shock.

Married? No way in hell would a person with half a brain believe *we* were married. He was . . . he was . . . and I was . . . I looked up at him, trying to read his expression in the dimly lit yard. He refused to look at me.

"But we're really sick of each other's company. You know

how it is." I bit my lip to keep from laughing. Beside me, Will grew quiet and, if possible, stiffer. What the hell did he expect?

If there was one thing I'd learned from my days on the road, it was that if we stayed, socialized, and drank a beer, they'd forget about us by morning. If we ran off, they'd probably be talking about us for days. The odds were fifty-fifty. "We could use a break."

"Well, come on over and get a beer." She grabbed my hand, dragging me from Will's embrace. "I'm Katie."

Will cleared his throat. I turned and rolled my eyes at him. *How dumb do I look?* "I'm Deanna."

Kate got us both beers, then introduced Will to a few of the guys before dragging me off to chairs strategically placed around the stairs. They led up to a deck that seemed to circle the entire doublewide trailer. An assortment of women clustered around the foot of the stairs talking and drinking beer.

I had to give credit where it was due. Will knew how to blend in. He talked and laughed, sipped his beer, and occasionally threw me a smoldering look that had Kate nudging me and laughing as well.

"You're gonna get it when you get home, girl."

She had *no* idea. Will probably was going to beat me. Or at the least, think about it.

A couple of the other women laughed. I have to admit that, from here, I guess Will did look like any other guy. Except older. Today he'd dressed in faded jeans and a T-shirt (that was now a sadly wilted shadow of its former sharply creased self) and battered Nikes, and his hair was still mussed from his earlier nap. Even the way he laughed at something one of the other men said seemed normal. I fell, right then and there, into a fantasy where Will and I really were on our honeymoon, married, *normal.*

And *not* hunted.

11

Will hated being out here in the open, hated the noise, hated the rowdy crowd that prevented him from keeping an eye on things. He hated feeling so vulnerable. But it was a relief not to be alone with Sabrina anymore.

She also made him feel vulnerable but in a different way. Her accusatory looks had been replaced with curious ones. He'd never in all his thirty-some years had anyone ask the questions she'd asked. People either didn't know what he did or accepted his job at face value, and respected his profession enough to leave it alone. His reputation usually spoke for itself—but then, she didn't know that. She kept staring at him, the questions she kept asking him . . . hell, the questions he'd asked her. He had no business digging into her past. Just like he had no business reading her journals.

Will raised his beer bottle to Sabrina.

"So what brings you to Buckshot Lake?" The question pulled Will's attention back to his present company.

"Honeymoon."

"You could have picked someplace nicer," another guy said with a laugh.

"But not as cheap," a third guy said, and a couple of them snickered.

Will hadn't bothered memorizing names, though he probably should have. He'd scanned all the faces, though, and they all seemed like locals. No outsiders—except for him and Sabrina. He glanced her way again, convinced he needed to keep an eye on her.

He wondered what in the hell Sabrina was telling those women. They laughed and clinked beer bottles. Not that he didn't trust her to be discreet, but what if they told conflicting stories? Luckily guys didn't usually care how you met a woman, just that she was good in bed. He listened with half an ear as they discussed their plans for water skiing and more beer drinking tomorrow.

"You ski, Roy?"

"Used to, when I was young." He smiled serenely, thinking he had at least ten years on every guy here, and turned his attention back to Sabrina. *What in the hell was she saying that had them laughing so hard?*

And she was laughing the loudest of them all. Not that it was a bad sound, but she was practically doubled over. It was almost embarrassing . . . and sort of cute.

She wiped at her eyes and gave him a little finger wave.

She stood out from the crowd, like she probably always did, in her wild skirt, her crazy hair, and dozens of bracelets. The snug white shirt she wore hugged her breasts as they jiggled with more laughter.

She glanced at him again and held his gaze, almost shyly before she turned away, sipping at her beer. He swallowed hard and glanced down when something jangled near his feet. Scamp.

"Your dog?" one guy asked. He was young and buff, and

had spent a lot of time flexing his muscles for the women on the porch to admire. And drinking a lot of beer. He looked like he thought he owned the world. Will had news for him. He didn't. Five minutes in the bushes and Will could prove it to him. Old man or no. And besides, by the time he was Will's age, he'd probably be fat and sloppy from all that beer.

"He's hers."

Scamp glanced over at Sabrina then settled at Will's feet, scratching behind his ear. Will sighed and shrugged at the younger man, and all of them laughed.

"Better than a cat."

"Remember when Jami's cat pissed on your best shirt?"

Then they were off again, reminiscing about shit Will didn't give a damn about. He scanned the trees, wondering how long they had, how long they'd be safe before they'd need to run again. They should probably leave soon, but he wasn't ready. Something was keeping him here. He glanced down at the dog at his feet.

Sabrina was keeping him here. Her presence here, with him, kept him from doing his own investigating—and hunting. His concern for her welfare was going to get them both killed.

Mr. Young and Buff wandered up to the porch.

He grabbed another beer from the cooler and said something to the women. A few laughed, but Katie said something Will couldn't quite catch. Whatever it was, the youngster didn't like it.

Judging from the frown and the stiff set of her shoulders, Sabrina didn't like what was going on either.

Will got no more than a step toward them when a voice stopped him. "I wouldn't."

It was Dewey or Dennie or something.

"Why not?"

"Katie and Tweeter always get into it."

"You could almost set your watch by it," someone else quipped, and they all laughed.

Up on the porch Sabrina set her beer down. She scowled, said something to Tweeter and flipped her hair over her shoulder.

Tweeter responded, and placed his foot on the bottom step. Unwilling to wait and see how it all played out, Will moved. Katie pushed past Sabrina and positioned herself between her and Tweeter. Her body language didn't speak, it screamed.

Hands on her hips, Katie proceeded to chew Tweeter out. ". . . the hell you think you are, but you don't own me. Matter of fact, last time I checked you were screwing around with Jami Lee. Stupid motherfucker."

Will couldn't see the younger man's face, but he didn't need to. Tweeter's stiff neck, clenched hands, and bunched shoulder muscles said plenty. The expression on Sabrina's face was a cross between anger and fear: two emotions that could make people do crazy-strange things. Will moved closer, ready to pull her out of whatever mess she was about to get herself into, but he wasn't fast enough.

Tweeter yanked Katie down the last few steps. She lost her balance and flew to the ground, landing on her knees as Sabrina quickly followed, positioning herself between the couple.

Around them, no one else seemed disturbed by the fight. A few women had even backed away, possibly looking for a quieter place to continue their conversation. As far as Will knew, the guys were still behind him, semi-hidden by the shadows, still making their plans for tomorrow and watching the goings-on. You might be able to set your watch by Katie and Tweeter, but Sabrina didn't know that.

"Don't you dare touch her again." Sabrina was right in the younger man's face, her hands propped on her hips, her own face contorted with emotions Will never thought he'd see from her. Besides the fear and anger there was... something dark and personal. She'd always struck him as so mellow and even-tempered. Even the anger she'd directed at him had been very matter of fact. But this... *this* was something different, something powerful that Will couldn't quite wrap his brain around.

"Deanna."

She ignored him while Katie struggled to her feet. Up on the porch, a few women chuckled, more turned away, someone grabbed a fresh beer from the cooler and tossed the cap in the garbage as if what was happening around them was commonplace.

"It's okay," the younger girl said, brushing herself off.

"No, it's not."

"*Deanna*," Will said again. He grabbed Sabrina by the upper arm. "Sweetheart. Let's go."

"No, Will. You go," she ground out, her voice thick and shaky with emotion.

"*We're* going." He kept his voice low and easy as he pulled at her arm, but she didn't budge. "Now."

"You're a pig. You make me sick. There's a special place in hell for pigs like you." Her voice rose with every sentence until finally the people around them seemed to realize that something interesting was going on. Spit landed on the younger man's shirt.

"It's okay. Really." The girl patted Sabrina's back and nudged her toward Will with a nod. "We do this all the time."

He had a feeling that sentiment wouldn't give Sabrina any comfort. He yanked harder this time, willing to incur her wrath if it would get her moving. Scamp whined, then barked and finally, Sabrina moved. Albeit slowly. She never took her eyes off Tweeter as Will led her into the trees.

"I should have killed him," she muttered under her breath as the lights from the party faded. It was just them making their way in the dark. A couple hundred yards and they'd be back at the cabin.

He knew how she felt about killing, so her words surprised him. He chastised her anyway. "You should have stayed out of it."

"Stayed out!" She spun around to face him, her expression unreadable in the shadows but her anger loud and clear.

The woods around them fell silent, and from the party came the sound of Stevie Ray Vaughn and laughter.

"We can't get involved, Sabrina."

"*You* get involved all the time."

"You *know* what I mean."

"No, goddamnit, I don't. Why don't you explain it to me?" Her voice broke as she huffed, struggling against tears Will sensed but couldn't see.

He swung her around, grabbed her free arm and pulled her close, speaking softly in case anyone had followed them. "We can't afford to be remembered, Sabrina. I may get involved, but people don't remember me. People are going to remember you because you stuck your nose in where it didn't belong."

"He was going—"

"I don't care." He leaned in closer until he could smell the beer on her breath and the warm saltiness of her tears, and finally understood why she was so upset. This had something to do with her mother's death. He gently squeezed her shoulders, silently willing her to relax, to understand. "All I care about is keeping you alive. And I can't do that if people remember you. *Us.*" He loosened his grip ever so slightly, silently praying she'd understand the possible ramifications of her actions tonight.

"I'm . . . sorry." She sniffed and wet her lips with the tip of her tongue, then blew out a damp breath. She finally looked at him. "I—"

Will wasn't listening, though. He was too busy focusing on her lips, on the warmth of her skin under his fingertips, on the tiny cocoon they seemed to have created out there in the middle of nowhere. He couldn't take his eyes from her mouth.

The need to kiss her twisted his gut, hardened his cock, hypnotized him. Seduced him with a quickness he couldn't fight as he leaned down and pressed his mouth to the lush, damp fullness of hers. He slid his hands up to cup her face only to find himself momentarily distracted by the softness of the curls that wound themselves around his fingers, caressed his hands, tempted him, tantalized him with images of Sabrina wearing nothing but her hair.

Finally, his hands connected with the downy soft skin of her face and she opened her mouth under his, her tongue darting to join his with an electrical jolt that had him jumping away.

He leaned against a tree, staring at her. Sabrina was off limits. Sabrina was *very* off limits. Never mind his abominable track record with women; sleeping with Sabrina was the most horrible idea he'd ever had.

Unfortunately, it'd be hours before his dick got the memo.

Today is the absolute best day of my life!

Will checked the date at the top of the entry. It read June 25, 2003. Sabrina currently lay snoring softly in the bed while Will sat in the van reading yet another journal with the help of a flashlight.

We're in Reno and we're getting married. I've never felt as close to anyone as I do Ronnie. But I'm scared. What if I end up like my mom? Ronnie says I'm nothing like her. That we won't be like them. He loves me too much. He says we can have kids, and as many dogs and cats as I want. He says we'll live in Denver with his mom until he gets out of the Army. I haven't met her, but he says she'll love me. Sometimes I pinch myself. I've never felt so safe.

As much as he didn't want to keep reading, Will couldn't resist. It was like rubbernecking at a car wreck: he couldn't turn away despite the sick, anxious twist of his stomach.

What was it that had driven Sabrina away from someone who'd loved her so much, who'd pledged to take care of her, adore her, cherish her? Someone who had obviously made her happy.

He turned pages, skimming through days and weeks of entries about Sabrina's blissful happiness with Ronnie and his mom, who sounded as if she was June Cleaver's clone. Or at least Carol Brady minus the six kids, since apparently Ronnie Hoffman was an only child and his momma's pride and joy.

By the time Will reached the end of the journal, he was still wondering what had happened to Ronnie—and more important, his marriage to Sabrina. But the last few pages were blank. The few entries before that were filled with blissful, happy, inane chatter about getting ready for Ronnie to come home on leave from the military and the big family Thanksgiving they were planning.

He stared at the book in his hand, running his fingers down the blank page as if he could magically fill them, as if he could uncover some hidden code to make the words appear. But of course, nothing did appear. And whatever had happened to Ronnie had pushed Sabrina out on the road again.

Maybe he'd died.

That had to be it. He'd died and left Sabrina alone, and his mother, maybe she'd really hated Sabrina. Pretended to like her for Ronnie's sake. Once Ronnie was dead—*What in the name of all that was fucking holy was he doing?*

He mentally shook himself and replaced the journal in its crate before quietly closing the van's side door.

Inside the cabin, Sabrina was still curled up in bed, a fist tucked under her chin, sweaty curls stuck to her face.

He stared down at her, wondering how he could know a perfect stranger as well as he felt he knew her. How could he know her better than he'd known Tilly, whom he'd lived with for nearly two years?

Was that even really possible? Really and truly possible? Or had he lost his mind?

Then again his relationship with Tilly had been based on lies. Maybe that was why John didn't lie. Lying made things so difficult, having to keep the lies straight, having to decide how much to lie about, if it was necessary to lie, having to remember whom you told what lie to. They all caught up with you in the end.

One way or the other.

No wonder lying made him so edgy and cranky. He didn't particularly *like* lying, but it came with the territory. With Sabrina, though, there had been no lies, no pretense, not after their initial meeting. There hadn't been a chance. In a way, they were kindred souls ... or was Will reaching? Was he seeing things that weren't there as a way to explain their earlier kiss? Scamp shifted and snuffled, digging for purchase in the soft blankets.

The sun would be up soon. With that thought in mind, he forced himself to move, to step away from the bed before Sabrina woke up and caught him staring. But he couldn't stop thinking about her, about that kiss, as he headed for the freezer. It was barely six in the morning, but he was starving. He felt edgy, and needed to stay busy. He pulled out some frozen, premade chicken-fried steak patties and stuck them in the oven, then he whipped up the gravy mix that had come with it and scrambled some eggs, all while his mind focused on Sabrina and the kiss they'd shared last night. He should have kissed her again. Ignored his conscience—and his ego. The irony of a hit man afraid of intimacy and miserably bad at it wasn't lost on him. Women scared him. Sabrina scared him. The thought of leaving her disappointed and angry terrified him.

While she slept and he did his best to imitate cooking, night slowly bled into day. He debated whether to wake Sabrina or not, then decided to leave her be. The last few days had been hard on her.

He was going soft, melting like a stick of butter left in a hot summer kitchen too long. He knew it, he could feel it, but he couldn't bring himself to care, to stop it, or even to stop her from getting to him.

He busied himself as long as he could, then ate with only a tattered copy of *Deer Hunter* magazine for company.

Finally, Scamp got up, barking a sharp little "See you later" at the open door before stepping outside and disappearing into the morning.

Will washed the dishes and left Sabrina's plate on the stove. He finally gave into the urge to check on her and wandered near the bed. Calf-length leggings hugged the lush curves of her body, and her white T-shirt, pulled tight from her restless sleep, was bunched up to reveal the swell of her belly and clung to her full breasts. She was braless, and through the thin material, Will could see the mouthwatering shadow of her areolas, the seductive shadow of soft nipples. His breath hitched as he wiped his sweaty hands on his jeans.

12

I came awake slowly, fighting the weighed-down feeling of struggling to break the surface after an especially deep dive. I was hot and sweaty, my head hurt and bad dreams lingered at the corners of my consciousness like that last slice of cake you gobble then wish you hadn't. For reasons I couldn't explain, mostly because I didn't understand them, I wanted to cry.

Then I looked up and found Will staring at me with all the lust and longing of a fat kid who'd just found his next sugar rush. For a second I thought I was dreaming. I closed my eyes until the sound of a heavy sigh reached my ears, then snuck another look from between my lashes.

To be honest, there was something kind of sweet about it, and I was afraid to move. Afraid I'd break whatever spell he was caught in. At the same time, I wanted to reach up, take him by the hand, and pull him down next to me. I wanted to shimmy out of the sweaty tangle of my clothes, use him, and let him use me. It had been way too long since I'd used sex as something more than a commodity.

Blood thickened in my veins, and heat pooled between my thighs and left me tender and achy. My nipples hardened against the damp confines of my T-shirt.

Groaning, Will turned away. It had to be the nipples. He was so lost in thought, he hadn't realized I was awake. He ran his hands through his hair and rubbed the back of his neck, exhaling heavily as he headed toward the front door. He stepped outside, leaving a trail of sunshine to spill across the floor and tempt me.

I tried to think about the consequences of sleeping with Will. But reason was blotted out by the memory of that naked, hungry look on his face.

As silently as possible, I sat up, my nose catching the distinct odor of pepper and frozen food that had been heated up. It's a funny smell, hard to pinpoint, hard to describe, but eat enough of it and you know it when you smell it. I must have slept the morning away. No surprise, since I'd spent most of the previous night staring at the ceiling and thinking about the kiss Will and I had shared, and how he'd run away like a sixteen-year-old unsure of what to do with his first real boner.

I felt certain that, when it came to his work, Will was as cold blooded and efficient as my initial impression of him. I felt equally certain that, when it came to the fairer sex, Will Collier didn't know jack shit.

I threw back the covers and slid from the bed, crossing the floor as silently as possible. Will sat still as a statue on the top step. The morning sun picked up the deep red glints in his short, normally immaculate hair, and he was still wearing yesterday's clothes. I bet he hadn't shaved yet either. Some perverse part of me liked the fact that I'd managed to shake loose the cold-blooded stuffed shirt and get a peek at what was underneath.

Smiling at the thought, I knelt behind him and untucked his plain gray T-shirt free of his shorts. He stiffened the tiniest but didn't protest as I lifted it over his head. I tossed it behind me, letting it land somewhere just inside the cabin.

Will's back was hard and smooth to the touch; all angles and planes and muscle that quivered under my fingertips. I pulled off my own T-shirt and pressed myself against him. The feel of skin on skin increased the ache that invaded me, pushed me onward, encouraged me to ignore the possibility of getting caught by someone, anyone, out here in the middle of nowhere. My nipples puckered against the skin of his back and a soft, damp breeze cooled me.

Will shivered, but he still hadn't moved. He didn't make a sound—of encouragement or dismissal. I let my hands explore every bare inch of him, the smooth almost hairless expanse of his chest, the stomach that quivered under my fingers, the nipples that stiffened under my fingertips. Finally, he grunted, moaned, a whoosh escaping his lungs before he could stop it. He turned, that same hungry, covetous look on his face, and leaned in, pressing his lips to mine.

I'd expected hard, demanding, and greedy. Instead, what I got was soft, but still hungry in a way I couldn't put my finger on. I pushed the thought out of my head and kissed him back, stroking his tongue with mine, drunk on my seduction, on the feel of the morning air on my skin, drunk on him and our kiss that threatened to swallow me whole.

Cocooned in our warm steamy bubble, we finally came up for air. "You sure?" Will studied me, his expression hopeful.

I gently caressed the side of his face. "I wouldn't be here if I wasn't."

"You said you hated me." His hand glided up my waist, kneading flesh.

"I still hate you." *Just not in the same way.* Now, I hated how he made me feel. I pushed away and shimmied out of my panties, sure he wouldn't turn down what I was offering as I held my hand out to him. "Now come on. Let's go inside."

13

Will let Sabrina lead him inside, seduced by the sight of her generous naked backside. She made him think of Eve in the garden as she glanced over her shoulder at him. Her eyes were hot and dark, her lips swollen from their kiss. The smell of sex filled his nose, intoxicating him until he was sick with need and numb with uncertainty. All the times he'd disappointed Tilly nibbled at the edges of his mind as he stood by the bed, letting Sabrina undress him; letting her kiss him and touch him.

She boldly wrapped her fingers around his cock and he watched, detached and fascinated, as it swelled, engorged with blood, aching from her attention. His balls followed suit, flexing and tightening against his body, preparing to release the semen gathered there. He almost forgot to breathe, then moaned and looked away, unable to watch her hand slide up and down his cock anymore. He was afraid he'd blow his wad way too early as the urge to come grew so strong he couldn't ignore it. He moaned again and pushed her hand away, embarrassed at his lack of control or finesse.

He wanted to touch her, but like a starving man presented

with a feast, didn't know where to start. His mouth dried out, and he struggled to swallow as Sabrina crawled onto the rumpled sheets. Her backside was deliciously round and full, a sight to behold naked, almost as nice as the front, which she presented to him, rolling over and reclining on the pillow, legs spread.

Still, he couldn't move. He watched her touch herself, her fingers dipping between her thighs. The wet sound of her playing with her pussy teased him, begging him to come closer and play, too. The fingers of her other hand teased her nipple and it hardened, puckered, dark and juicy like a ripe piece of fruit.

He felt like he was suffocating, smothering in the banquet she'd laid out for him. His cock urged him forward, begging for the release he'd find between Sabrina's thighs while the rest of him screamed something about him crossing a very dangerous line and possibly making a fool of himself. He was torn and confused. The sight of Sabrina now with her eyes closed, her lower lip caught between her teeth, moaning, smiling. Now her head was arching back, her hips jutting upward as she continued to stroke herself. He backed away, only to stop when she looked up at him with those liquid eyes and said his name.

"Come on," she coaxed, a languid smile on her face. She'd stopped playing with herself and held a wet finger out to him.

Finally, he moved, diving for the bed, wrapping his hand around her wrist, plunging her finger into his mouth. He licked her warm, salty juices while his cock screamed at him to fuck her.

His cock was a pig, with no manners.

There was so much he wanted to taste and touch, smell and see, he didn't know where to start. He was drowning in curves and an abundance of warm flesh as he found a nipple pressed against his lips. He opened his mouth and drew it in. She wriggled underneath him, and her hands were on his cock again, guiding him inside her soft, slick warmth. Then she was moving under him, and he was pumping into her. He kept his eyes closed, his face buried between the lush mounds of her breasts as his cock exploded, and he wanted to shout his frustration.

He didn't want it to be over, didn't want it to end, didn't want to see *the look* in Sabrina's eyes. The angry, disappointed look.

Instead, she laughed soft and hoarse. "Roll over."

Will kept his eyes closed, his fists clutching the sheets as she covered his body with hers. Sabrina's hips worked furiously, pushing her toward her own release. She pressed her lips to his ear, nipping and licking and purring. Finally, she squealed, a sharp sweet sound, and threw her head back, lips curved into a satisfied smile as her pussy pulsated around him.

Will sucked in great gulps of air and stared absently at the water-stained ceiling while he played with her hair, twisting curls around his fingers. Warmth and sexual release had him drifting off, his eyes refusing to stay open any longer.

He woke a while later to find Sabrina curled up against him spoon-fashion. He said a silent "thank you" that she hadn't mentioned his disappointing performance.

He caressed her back, letting his finger trace the dip of her waist and the rise of her hips. He cupped the half-moon of her ass, his cock stirring as her hips arched, curling into his hand, pressing against him. He wanted her with a fierceness that startled him, but he didn't look too closely at it. Not now. He was busy.

Instead, he slid his cock inside her, sighing as his belly clenched. He wrapped his arms around her and pumped into her pussy, his face buried in her hair. The thought of waking up like this every day left him dizzy. Or maybe it was just lack of blood to his head, but the sweet, slick feel of Sabrina milking his cock . . . He groaned, "You feel so good!"

She gurgled and gasped, deep throaty sounds that made his balls ache, and undulated against him, meeting his cock stroke for stroke. She shifted against him, a little harder, a little faster. The slap of skin against skin reached his ears, and her nails dug into his ass, urging him on. It felt good, that little edge of pain, sharp and bittersweet mixed with his pleasure. She moaned again, urging him to hurry.

"I don't wanna hurry; I don't wanna stop, Bree."

Her hot, sweet pussy drew him on, teasing him, tormenting him until her head rolled back and his lips were on her cheek. She groaned loudly, smiling as her cunt spasmed around him repeatedly, dragging him along for the ride. Will came with a shout, his face buried in her neck. He held on tight until the aftershocks faded away, until her pussy stopped pulsating around him. Until he thought he could act like a semi-coherent man again.

He brushed the hair from her sweaty cheek and kissed her temple.

"What a way to waste a day." Her lips curved into a smile.

Will laughed, a part of him feeling silly and foolish for being unable to take his eyes off her and for not knowing how to respond.

That hadn't been half bad. Well, *he* hadn't been half bad... or rather, he'd been better than normal. Better than he could recall in recent memory.

"Where'd you go?" Sabrina asked, curling up against him. She rested her head on his chest.

"I'm here." He smiled, unable to help himself.

"Can I ask you something?"

His heart immediately seized up in his chest. Was she going to ask the dreaded *how did he feel about her* or *where did they go from here*? "What?"

"Why..." She propped herself up on her elbows so she could see him. Curls hid most of her face, but not her eyes, which were now a deep green. "Why do you"—she hesitated, licked her lips. Finally, she met his gaze head on—"kill people? Really."

This was the second time she'd asked him about his work, and her question was the reason he always lied. He felt as if someone had just sucked the life right out of him. He briefly squeezed his eyes shut and forced his shoulders to relax. There was no easy answer, none that would ever satisfy her. And there was no way this conversation would end well. "It's my job."

Her eyebrows drew together slightly, and she struggled to sit up. "It's not just a job. You . . . *take* human lives! Those people, they matter to someone. They have lovers and families . . . children!"

Air finally filled Will's lungs, and he exhaled heavily as realization dawned. This wasn't about him, not really. This was about her mother and Walt. He nodded to himself in understanding. "Can I ask *you* something?"

"I suppose," she said softly, her eyes wary.

"How did your mom die?" He sat up while he waited for her to answer. Sweat trickled down his back and made the sheets stick to his legs.

"My stepfather shot her."

Even though he'd suspected as much, his chest still constricted slightly when she said it. He sighed and waited to see if she'd continue.

"I was at work. They, uh, they were fighting when I left. . . ."

"About the baby?" The words were out of his mouth before he could stop them. He fisted the sheets, a part of him hoping she'd miss his slip, but he knew it was hopeless.

Sabrina lurched across the bed, settling on her haunches. All the blood seemed to have drained from her face. "You read my journal?" The soft tone of her voice scared him more than if she had yelled. "How dare you! How *dare* you!"

He swallowed the lump in his throat, scrambling for the right words. "I'm sorry," was the best he could do. He sat up and scrubbed at his head.

"Fuck... *Will*, how could you read my journal?" She scowled at him. Her eyes widened and her brows slowly rose as she added, "*Journals?*"

He nodded.

"How many? How much do you know?"

Now was not the time to lie. "Three or four. I know about... Ronnie. Well, not everything, because you didn't finish."

"I'm so *sorry* to *deprive* you!" She climbed from the bed and snatched up her clothes, clutching them to her chest. "I'm—"

"Ask me anything!" He cut her off, unwilling to hear her say how angry she was, how much she hated him or that she was leaving him.

Her shoulders slumped, and the clothes slipped from her fingers to land on the edge of the bed. She daintily slid on her panties before asking the first question, "What's the point? Why should I bother?"

"I figured it was only fair. Since I know so much about you."

"You don't know shit about me." She pawed at the covers until she came up with something to hold her wild hair back with.

"Why don't you settle down somewhere, get off the road? Don't you want a normal life?"

"Ha! Normal! Coming from you that's—" She shook her head, then perched on the end of the bed and exhaled a noisy breath. "You get paid to kill people for a living. What's normal about that? What's normal about *your* life?"

She had him there.

His face burned as humiliation and resignation settled deep in his gut. "Nothing. But it is what it is and I am what I am,

Bree. And lying is a part of the job." His shoulders slumped with the weight of it. "But you know what? I'm *tired*, and that's no lie. I'm tired of the traveling, the lying, the secrecy, the multiple identities. Most of all, I'm tired of trying to keep it all straight. It makes me dizzy sometimes. You're the only woman I never . . . *almost* never lied to."

"Well, isn't that special! Should I feel all honored and shit?"

He shook his head. He had no one to blame but himself, but he'd known this wouldn't end well. "I'm going to take a shower."

14

Nothing kills a postcoital glow like reality.

"Well, wasn't that exciting?" I muttered. Staring at the bathroom door, I wondered how long Will was going to hide in there. Even though I knew it was impossible, a part of me hoped he'd drown. I was still seething over him reading my journals!

Scamp appeared next to the bed and stared up at me, his head tilted slightly to the side.

"What, dude?" I reached down and gave him a scratch.

I didn't want to think about my mom or my stepdad, who'd gotten away with murder, or Ronnie, who'd finished up his tour in Afghanistan, then died in a car crash on the way home from the airport. All of it was enough to give a girl a complex. Nothing ever went like I planned, so I'd stopped planning, learned to improvise and go with the flow, and settling down had just seemed like a bad idea after Ronnie.

Nothing ever worked out. Not even this, here with Will.

I was finished. I sank onto the edge of the bed, my T-shirt fisted in my hands, my eyes on the bathroom door.

Scamp barked once, then trotted toward the front door and

back again. I glanced at the bathroom door. My heart picked up speed, tapping steadily against my ribs as I grabbed a clean pair of jeans out of my bag and slid into them. "You ready to blow this popsicle stand?"

He barked again and danced toward the door.

I couldn't... wouldn't... stay here any longer.

Will had had his two days. And the sex had been fun. Despite Will's initial... slip, I'd actually been looking forward to more.

Oh well, it wasn't like he'd be stranded here. He had a cell phone; he could call someone. Besides, I had no intention of sitting in this cabin staring at him any longer, knowing that he knew all the things... humiliation made my cheeks burn. I left the thought unfinished. There'd never be a better time to run.

Glancing at the bathroom door again, I decided if I was going to leave, I should get my ass in gear. I was unused to leaving fate in someone else's hands and tired of hiding. I packed up my stuff, slowed by hands clumsy with fear. Grabbing Will's jeans from the floor, I went fishing for the keys to my van, but they weren't there. I suppose that would have been too easy.

I dove into one of his bags, then the other, digging around until I finally came out a winner.

"Come on, Scamp." My own bag slung over my shoulder, I darted out the door. My heart pounded in my chest; the keys were slippery in my sweaty hands. Will would kill me if he caught me. Maybe not literally, but he'd want to.

I scooped Scamp up and threw him into the van along with my bag and climbed in. Slamming the door, I shoved the key in the ignition.

The engine turned over but didn't catch. "Please start, please, *please* start!" I pumped the gas a few times, praying I didn't flood it, and tried again, but it still didn't catch. Now all of me was shaking, and Scamp danced around in the passenger seat.

The achingly hot steering wheel was slippery against my palm. "Yeah, I know, dude. I'm trying!"

I slammed the door lock down with my elbow, praying if Will came out, he'd go for my door and not one of the others as I tried yet again. The engine whined, struggling to catch.

A "Hey!" sounded from outside the van.

My heart caught in my throat at the sight of Will in the sideview mirror. He stood on the porch in nothing but a towel, a scowl on his face.

"Please God, let it start! Please, please, please," I whispered. I tried one last time, almost sick with relief as the engine roared to life. Hot air came gushing out the vents and sweat trickled down my sides. I threw the gearshift in reverse and hit the gas, flying past Will, who darted down the porch steps, that tiny towel clutched around his waist. The edge flapped like a flag in the breeze.

"God *damnit*, Bree, *stop*!"

I should have known about the journal when he'd called me Bree that second time in bed. I shut out the visual of us having sex spoon-fashion. I didn't need those sorts of distractions right now.

I glanced back, hit with a brief pang of conscience, but stopping was not on my agenda. I threw the van into drive and took off down the dirt road toward town.

Twenty agonizing, gut-wrenching minutes later, I breezed through the tiny town of Buckshot, Texas, population 3,129, my eye on the speedometer. The last thing I needed at this point was to get stopped by the cops for speeding—real or imagined.

Once I crossed the county line, I breathed a sigh of relief. There was no way Will could catch me. I'd left him in the middle of nowhere with no transportation. But he was a resourceful guy. He'd be fine.

And so would I.

* * *

The summer sun was on the downward slope and doing its best to scorch my eyelids by the time I crossed the Travis County line. Austin meant I was on the home stretch of my drive. I forced my stiff shoulders to relax and my brain to start working again.

First thing first, I locked away all thoughts of Will. There was no sense in looking back.

"Back is just a waste of time, right, Scamp?" He didn't answer, but then, I didn't really keep him around for his conversational abilities.

Second, San Antonio seemed the most logical place to go. I couldn't afford to piss away the seven-hundred-and-fifty-dollar vendor fee I'd paid. I *really* needed the money, winter would be here before I knew it, and there were only a couple of big fairs left this season. With the price of gas, I'd need to stockpile all the cash I could, then find a place to hole up. Maybe get a job waitressing in some tiny diner, maybe get an apartment.

"Something nice." I glanced at Scamp, who had his head resting on his paws. Someplace that allowed dogs.

With one last glance in the rearview mirror, I set the cruise control and turned up the radio, singing along with Snow Patrol.

I'd settle down for a little while. Nothing permanent, though—I didn't *do* permanent; just through the winter.

15

Will stood at the edge of the driveway cursing a blue streak. His feet were coated with red sandy loam from running through the driveway to the road, and sore from the gravel digging into his feet. He coughed from the dust Bree's van had left in its wake. "Fuck!"

She'd played him. *Totally and completely played him.* Fucked him to get away from him.

He'd made an amateur mistake of the worst kind: He'd let his guard down.

Swearing again, he turned back toward the cabin and hobbled inside. She'd left a mess: clothes from his bags were strewn everywhere. Will grabbed the disposable cell phone then threw it down in disgust. It was dead and his charger didn't fit; he'd already tried.

He rifled through his stuff until he found his own phone and plugged it in. He slammed the cabin door, rinsed his feet off, then got dressed and packed up his stuff. Just long enough for his phone to charge.

Will dialed Wynn's number, wondering how long it would

take his brother to come get him. And how much shit he'd get for his fuckup.

A recording of Julie's cheerful voice greeted him. "Hi, we can't get to the phone right now. Leave a message."

"Fuck . . . fuck, fuck, fuck, fuck, *fuck*!" His grip tightened on the cell phone, and he almost threw it. Only the thought of being stuck with no way to get help stopped him. He tried Wynn again, in case they were screening their calls, but had no luck. Next he tried his brother John, who answered on the third ring. John was the last person Will wanted to ask for help, but he had to get the fuck out of this cabin. He had to find out who was hunting him and stop them before they found Bree. He couldn't do it stuck in the middle of nowhere.

"Hello."

Will gritted his teeth and forced himself to speak. "I need help."

John snorted.

"Don't be an asshole. I need you to come get me. Where are you?"

"In Austin, looking for you."

"Fuck."

"You forgot to check in with Mom."

Will groaned and sank down at the kitchen table. How the hell could he have forgotten? "I know."

"Wow, did Wee Willie fuck up?"

"Don't be an asshole. And don't call Dad. Just come get me."

"Fine. Where are you?" was followed by something that sounded suspiciously like "dickhead."

Will told him, filling him in on everything but the fact he'd had sex with Sabrina. He'd *definitely* never hear the end of that.

"Why didn't you just let her go?"

"They would have killed her!"

"Not your problem."

Will didn't agree but kept his mouth shut. Arguing with John, who had to have the last word, was an exercise in futility.

"So how'd she get away?"

"I was sleeping."

John snorted again.

"I called Wynn, but he wasn't home." *You're my second choice* went unsaid.

"You didn't try Danielle," John said, referring to their baby sister.

"Don't be an ass. Are you going to come get me or not?"

"Call Mom." John hung up before Will had a chance to thank him. Not that he was feeling especially thankful. He had hours and hours and hours to kill, at least six or seven. Despite his anger, he was worried about Sabrina. The TV was iffy at best, and he had no radio to break the monotony of what was going to be a very long day.

Will checked his cell phone and discovered four missed calls from his mother. It was a wonder he didn't have more. *Lots more.* She usually restrained herself when she knew he was working, but once a job was over, well, she turned into a typical mother hen again, worrying about her chicks.

He cleared his throat, hoping he sounded normal. "Hi, Mom."

"Willie! Where on God's green earth have you been?"

"My phone was dead. I just now found it." Another reason he hated lying. His mother could sniff them out like that cartoon bear sniffed out picnic baskets. The one with the friend named Boo Boo.

She sighed loud and heavy in his ear. "*That woman's* been calling here."

"What?" *Which woman,* he was almost afraid to ask.

"Tilly. She says you have some of her stuff. I keep telling her you're out of town on business but . . ."

But Tilly could be like a dog with a bone when she wanted something. If he'd taken something of hers when he left, it hadn't been on purpose. "I'll come home next week and try to find whatever she's looking for."

"Now, how's Austin? Have you been down on Sixth Street drowning your sorrows in beer? You know she's not worth it. She never was good enough for you and frankly, Willie dear, I never liked her."

He rolled his eyes as a headache began to thump somewhere in the depths of his head.

"Willie? William!"

"Yes, Mom. No, not Sixth Street, just . . ." He sighed.

"I know it's hard, baby, but you'll find the right woman someday. A *good* woman. Now, pick yourself up and dust yourself off and put a smile on that beautiful face. Are you smiling?"

"Yes, Mom." And he was, however briefly.

"I expect to hear from you on Wednesday before I go play bridge."

"Yes, ma'am. I won't forget."

"I love you, baby. Chin up."

He hung up feeling guilty for lying but pleased he'd escaped their conversation relatively unscathed.

Will packed the last of his stuff and cleaned the cabin, cleaning being preferable to pacing or sitting. A fishing show punctuated by bursts of static and the occasional roar of an outboard engine from the nearby lake didn't do much for Will's sanity. He practically lunged for the phone when it rang a few hours later.

"I'm just north of Fort Worth," John said.

"Jesus! Could you drive any slower?" Will ran a hand through his hair, wondering how much more pacing he could do.

"Hey, fuck you! I can hang up now and not tell you about the text message I just got."

Will sank down on the bed, now made up with all the pillows and blankets in place. "Do I want to hear this?"

"Who the hell did you piss off?"

"Don't fuck with me, John. Not now."

"You didn't tell me everything, did you?"

"I told you what you needed to know."

"Well, someone seems to think that having your girl matters to me. Why is that?" Sarcasm. Lots of it.

Will ignored it, focusing on the bigger picture. They didn't think; they *knew* it would matter to him. Never mind that she'd run off and left him, he still had a responsibility to see that Sabrina didn't end up dead. He'd thought that going on the offensive, tracking down the killer, might be the way.

Apparently, someone had other plans. He'd failed miserably. He propped his head in his hand. "How did they get your number?" he croaked out.

"Who the hell knows, but you're lucky they didn't text Dad."

Like their dad even knew *how* to text. He could barely use his cell phone, but Will kept his mouth shut. "What did it say?"

"*The girl for your brother.*" John chuckled, dryly. "I have to say, with you out of the picture—"

"Less talk; more driving."

Three of the longest hours of his life later, headlights pierced the cabin's windows as a nondescript sedan pulled into the driveway.

His patience worn thin, Will shut the door behind him. The solitude, the hot cabin, and his worry over Bree had worn him to a frazzle.

"How the hell did you find this place?" John asked as he

climbed out and stretched, sunglasses firmly in place. With the same tall, broad-shouldered build and brown hair that only differed by a shade or two, they could have passed for twins, and had on more than one occasion.

"Julie. Some friend of a friend of hers." Will hefted his bags onto his shoulders. "Now let's go."

"Figures."

"What's that supposed to mean?" Will threw his bags in the back seat as John circled around to the passenger side.

"If anyone knows about getting lost, she does."

Ignoring his dig at their sister-in-law, who John disliked immensely (and vice versa), Will climbed in and fired up the sedan. "Let me see that text message." John handed over his phone and Will studied it. "Why would they send it to *you*?"

"Sounds like someone's attempt to make it personal."

"Did you try and call—"

"Of course." John glared at him, obviously insulted by Will's lack of faith at his abilities. "The number was no good."

Will spun the car around and headed back toward town.

"Where . . . are you going?"

"To find Bree."

"*Bree*," John breathed, a knowing smile on his face and eyebrows arched.

Will smothered a groan. "Don't start, please."

"You can't just take off all half-assed. You don't even know where to look."

"Matter of fact, I do." He'd had plenty of time to think about it while he waited. There weren't many places for Sabrina to run to, and he figured she'd been caught somewhere between here and San Antonio.

"So do I." John gave him a knowing smile.

Will slammed on the breaks and the car fishtailed, nearly ending up in a ditch before it came to a stop in a cloud of thick red dust. "For someone who can't lie to save his ass, you sure do know how to walk around it."

"I got another text message about an hour ago."

"And you were going to tell me this when?"

"She's just a girl."

"She's"—Will swallowed the lump in his throat—"she's not just a girl. She's my responsibility." Along with a bunch of other stuff he chose not to share with his brother. "What did the message say?"

"You didn't say we were playing Lone Ranger. You said come get you."

"*What did the message say?*" Will bit out from between clenched teeth.

"Noon tomorrow in San Antonio. Said you'd know where."

The Ren fair.

"I've got news." Wynn skipped over the niceties and got down to business as soon as he answered the phone, something Will appreciated.

"So do I," Will said.

"Want to go first?"

"It'll keep." Once they'd passed Gainesville, Will set the cruise control and stretched in his seat. His long day was far from over.

"Rumor has it that Dre Anderson is cleaning up after himself."

Sighing, Will hit the phone's speaker button so John could hear. "Dre Anderson, huh?"

"Yeah."

Will glanced at John, who shrugged. Dre had hired Will to take out Derek, his business partner. "I never wanted to take that job in the first place." He should have listened to his gut. Not that the job had felt wrong or difficult. Dre had been a referral, an acquaintance of an acquaintance. It happened all the time, and Will hadn't thought a thing about it beyond his gut, which had tried to warn him for reasons he'd never been able to put his finger on.

Chances were, Will hadn't received the last 1.5 million Dre owed him either. Bastard. "Any idea why?"

"No. Just cleaning house."

"He's a dead man," John muttered.

"John?" Wynn asked.

"Yeah," Will said. "Sabrina ran off. And apparently whoever Dre hired to tidy things up has caught up with her."

"Where are you?"

"Should be in Denton in about thirty minutes."

"Pick me up."

"Julie's not gonna like it." John smirked at Will, obviously happy to be a part of *anything* that Julie didn't like.

"I'll handle her. Let's just go get your girl back."

"She's not—"

John snorted again.

The line went dead.

They were south of Denton before Will spoke again, trying to work out the one piece of the puzzle that still niggled at him. "Why would they text you?"

"Where's your cell phone?"

Will groaned. "Shit. It was dead when I found it. I bought a disposable after the shooting and that's what I used to call Wynn."

"They might have texted you, but there in the boonies, I'm sure cell reception was sucky at best."

Struck with a horrible thought, Will's eyes narrowed on the three-lane highway. "Or."

"Or?"

"It's personal."

"Why would Dre make it personal?"

"He wouldn't, but the guy he hired might. Why else would he text you"—Will held up a finger—"besides my dead phone. This is someone who knew your cell phone number." And in their line of work, they didn't exactly walk around handing out business cards.

"You're right," John conceded. "What do you know?"

"Not much." Will shook his head, his attention divided by the thickening traffic. "Only that whoever he is, he had the Monte Carlo I used in Phoenix."

"So he had to have followed you."

"I was careful." Will scowled at John, his mind trying to sort it all out. He didn't do kids or women, he stayed out of domestic disputes, and he didn't go after connected families. "I'm *always* careful."

"I'm not saying you weren't."

At Wynn's house, Will skipped a late dinner in favor of a shower while John filled Wynn in on their earlier discussion in the car.

Will had just snapped the last button on his jeans and reached for a T-shirt when a knock sounded at the door. "Come in."

"How you holding up?" Julie slipped in the room and closed the door, all fresh-faced smiles, her brown hair falling over her shoulder.

He shrugged and sank down on the bed, pulling his shirt firmly into place. "Anxious to get going."

"You'd do better with some sleep. Matter of fact, the guys are talking about leaving in the morning, before sunup." Julie held up a hand when he started to protest. "It's obvious someone wants you more than her. She'll be okay. John's exhausted; you are, too. You look like you've been through the wringer."

"I'm worried," he softly confessed. Even though Wynn and

Julie had been married nearly a year, Will had spent so much of the last year working, he didn't know her that well. If it had been his sister, Danielle, he would have shot straight, but Julie he wasn't so sure about. That said, if Wynn trusted her, Will did, but... "I'm worried about Bree." He really had to stop calling her that. Using her nickname implied *things*... things that weren't there. Things he didn't want to think about—like steamy-hot, early-morning sex.

She sat on the bed next to him and draped an arm across his shoulder. "Tell me about her."

He shrugged and laughed, his throat thick with emotions completely unfamiliar to him as he started to talk.

"So her dad killed her mom," Julie said when he finally stopped talking.

"Stepdad," he corrected. "And yeah."

"No wonder she ran. That's pretty heavy-duty stuff there, bucko."

Will sighed, glancing over at the guest bedroom's tidy dresser. "Yeah. What if I don't—"

"You will. You Collier men know how to pinch hit." She laughed softly and patted his shoulder. "Leave your dirty clothes. I'll wash 'em."

16

I was so exhausted, I almost stopped for the night in Austin, but forced myself to push on, needing to get back to that last safe place I'd known. And as far as possible from Will, the cabin, and the bed we'd made love in.

Once I reached the fair, I showed the security guy my pass. He waved me in and mentioned the location of a few good spots.

I was still torn over whether going back to work was a good idea, then reminded myself that I was running dangerously close to broke. Maybe not in real-world terms but in Sabrina-land, less than a grand in the stash was unacceptable. And really, who the hell would look for me here, at the scene of the crime?

I parked the van between two campers—a pop up and a Winnebago—and made myself at home. Scamp knew better than to leave my sight, so I let him wander without his leash, sniffing tires and exploring our little temporary oasis. The fair would run for five more weekends. I could make some serious money. At least two grand, if I worked my ass off; then I could hit that fair in Baton Rouge—I'd already registered. That ran for two months. After that, I'd settle in somewhere warm for the winter, maybe Galveston. Some time near the ocean really appealed to me, even if the thought of being alone didn't. I chose not to examine who or what had caused my single state to up and decide to bother me.

I squirmed against the ache in my chest while thinking I'd had my fill of adventures... and dangerous men.

"Excuse me, miss?"

Inwardly groaning at the intrusion, I stood and peeked around the van's side door to find a hulking stranger holding Scamp. He wore what looked like a homespun shirt and vest over tan pants tucked into leather boots. Dark hair fell across his forehead, brown eyes twinkled from beneath thick brows, and the lower half of his face was covered in stubble. "This belong to you?"

Scamp licked his hand then gave me a stupid doggy grin.

"Yeah, sorry." I crossed to where he stood and took Scamp from him. "He hates the leash."

"I'm Jim."

"Sabrina."

Jim was tall, almost as tall as Will. I sighed, forcing him out of my head. Not *now*. Not anymore. I swallowed the lump in my throat. A part of me hoped Jim wasn't the talkative kind. I wasn't really in the mood.

"You just get in?"

"Yeah." I smiled, thinking to myself that I'd be fine. Really. Now I just had to make myself believe it.

"Buy you a turkey leg?" Jim offered.

From nearby came the sounds of a television, of cabinets slamming and pots and pans clanging. It reassured me that there actually were people nearby and reminded me that I hadn't eaten since... Lord, early this morning when I'd stopped to get gas.

I'd been so anxious to put as many miles as I could between Will and me, I hadn't stopped for anything more substantial than coffee and a bagel. "You working the fair? I don't recall seeing you around." Not that *I'd* been around, but Jim didn't need to know that.

"Yeah. I'm"—he pointed toward the fairgrounds—"working the rides."

The rides were low-tech and required good old-fashioned brute strength to run. I didn't envy him at all, but he looked more than up to the job.

"Gimme a minute." I grabbed Scamp's leash and locked up the van, pocketing the keys. We walked in silence for a few minutes. "How long you been working the fairs?"

"This is my first."

"I see." There were two kinds of people who worked Ren fairs: Those with a passion for all things Renaissance who lived for the few months when the fair came to town. And then there were the rest of us. Those who lived a non-conventional life, who didn't mind all the travel . . . like me. I loved what I did. Some of the real diehards even learned to joust and swordfight. Personally, I'd always had a yen to learn belly dancing, but I'd never gotten around to it.

This wasn't exactly the life I'd dreamed of, but it was mine and I owned it. "Where you from?"

"Here and there." Jim shrugged and smiled, slowing his gait to match mine.

"So you travel with the fairs? Or are you local?"

"*Newly* local." He gave me another grin, showing off his pearly white teeth. "I've always had a thing . . . and when I saw they were hiring." He shrugged almost sheepishly. "You?"

"I'm a traveler."

"Like a gypsy?" One thick eyebrow arched slightly. "You look like one."

"Yeah, like a gypsy. Except I'm *not*. I travel the fair circuit as many months of the year as I can."

We stood in line for turkey legs and lemonade for me and beer for him, then sat at the empty amphitheater. The crowd had dissipated, driven off by the heat and tired children even though things didn't officially shut down until sunset.

"So where you from, Sabrina?"

"New York."

"You don't sound like it." He picked off a piece of turkey and threw it to Scamp. Points for him.

Now it was my turn to smile sheepishly. "I haven't been back in . . . twelve years." I wouldn't call it home. Not in a *million* years.

"You don't look old enough to have been on your own for twelve years."

I shrugged and nibbled at my turkey leg. It wasn't really any of his business.

"I'm prying, aren't I?"

"Yeah." I nodded, glad he could take a hint.

"I didn't see you out working today? What do you do?"

"I read tarot cards and I . . . had some personal stuff to take care of."

"Oh." He nodded and, luckily for me, dropped the subject.

Halfway to the van, Jim grabbed my hand, wrapping it in his large callused one. "You sleeping here?" He nodded toward the van.

"Yeah." *But you're not, buddy!*

"You *are* a gypsy."

I shrugged, a part of me ready for him to leave, hoping he didn't think a turkey leg and lemonade bought him a night with me. He seemed nice enough, but my run-in with Will was still fresh in my mind. I wasn't ready to get involved, even casually, and Jim seemed like the type to get real pushy if he wanted something. Good thing I knew how to push back, if needed.

"I'll see you later." I freed my hand and backed away, dragging Scamp with me.

"Tomorrow?"

"Sure." Shrugging, I jammed a hand in my pocket and fished out my keys.

"Definitely." Nodding slowly, almost to himself, he gave me a once-over that left me shivering in its wake and wishing I hadn't agreed to see him tomorrow, even casually. He took a few steps back, disappearing into the gathering dusk.

"Tomorrow, maybe not," I murmured to Scamp.

He whined and walked in a circle.

Anxious to get settled in before it got fully dark, I unlocked the van and pulled the door open, my jaw dropping and heart plummeting as I stared from the door that I *knew* I'd locked to the van's interior. Around me, the early evening was eerily quiet, my neighbors suddenly nowhere to be found or maybe sleeping. A breeze shuddered past, thick with the scent of meat smoke and something bitter.

I'd locked the van, but that obviously hadn't kept someone out. My clothes and journals were scattered all over the place, and someone had even slashed my pillow. Foam stuffing was scattered everywhere like a pale yellow blizzard had struck. "Fuck . . . *me*."

Tears filled my eyes and, with a hiccup, I dove inside. I scrambled over the mattress and reached under the driver's seat. There was nothing there. The oversized vitamin bottle I stashed all my money in was gone. A whimper slipped past my lips. I sagged against the back of the seat. Eight hundred dollars gone. Gone.

God, maybe they hadn't found it! Maybe it was still here!

I spent the next thirty minutes setting the van to rights,

sweeping up all the foam and searching for the vitamin bottle but came up empty handed.

Other than the two twenty dollar bills in my pocket, I was broke.

I slumped against the side of the van, head in my hands. Good thing I'd planned on working tomorrow and Sunday. If I was lucky, I could pull in about six hundred dollars, but that was *incredibly* optimistic. I'd more likely pull four hundred. An extra job was no longer optional, but mandatory, and there'd be no splurging on hotels and hot showers while I was here. Not to mention food and kibble for Scamp, who was currently nowhere to be seen.

Terrified at the thought of losing Scamp, too, I lunged for the van's door and stuck my head outside. I collapsed with relief at the sight of him sitting on the ground, patiently waiting for me to remember he was there. "Sorry, boy."

I gently lifted him inside and slammed the door, clutching him to me in the stuffy darkness.

Right then, I wished I *was* back at the cabin, with Will, playing Go Fish and listening to the crickets chirp and asking him stupid questions he didn't want to answer. Maybe even . . . I sniffled . . . making love.

I stretched out on the mattress, Scamp held firmly in my grasp, and cried myself to sleep.

The following morning I woke up resigned to starting over, something I'd done so many times I'd lost count. I stretched and threw back the covers, pulling a T-shirt on before I opened the door and let Scamp out. I let him do his business, then trudged across the campground to the nearest bathroom to shower. I cleaned up and changed, then grabbed coffee and a roll from the cantina. That left me thirty-seven dollars. After feeding Scamp and myself, I changed into a gypsy skirt and peasant blouse and tied my hair back. It was nearly eight, and I had a long day ahead of me.

I'd no sooner gotten settled in my spot than Jim showed up. He still hadn't shaved, which, I suppose, made his Renaissance-style attire more authentic, and a little menacing. Today he wore baggy black pants tucked into his boots and a white shirt with blousy sleeves. It set off his tan and revealed some of his chest hair. The young mothers were going to *love* him.

He set a fresh cup of coffee on the table and said, "You look like you could use this."

"Thanks." Still feeling wary and raw after last night, I forced myself to smile. He struck me as the loner type, so I didn't *think* I'd been played; I didn't *think* he'd had an accomplice rob me while he fed me. And besides, if that was his game, there was definitely more lucrative pickings around here than me.

"Bad night?"

Nothing he needed to know about. "I had a hard time settling in. So do you own a house or rent?"

His eyes narrowed and he sat up a little on the tiny stool normally used by customers. "Why? Lookin' to move in?"

I laughed. "Not quite. I'm thinking of staying here, after the fair."

"Settling down, huh?" He crossed his arms on the table and leaned forward until his face was only a foot or so from mine.

My smile firmly in place, I leaned back, unwilling to let him or anyone else invade my personal space after the night I'd had. "Yeah."

"How about we celebrate with lunch, then? My treat."

"Jim, you don't have a jealous girlfriend lurking around here, do you?"

"No." He held up a hand. "Friends. Just friends. I'll come by around eleven thirty or so."

I watched him walk away while thinking at least it was a free meal.

Jesus Christ, what had I gotten myself into now?
Praying I didn't trip in the thick crowd, I glanced over my shoulder. Jim was hot on my tail.

Will hadn't lied. Not one itty bitty bit had he lied.

As I ran, my glimpses of Jim were few and far between. The bastard even flashed me a scary grin at one point.

I spun around and pushed my way through the crowd, determined to put as much distance between us as possible.

Will hadn't lied, and *I* was an idiot. *A world-class idiot.*

Jim had come by around 11:30 for lunch, looking obviously impatient by the way he'd paced around while I finished with a client.

"Everything okay?" I'd asked once she was gone. I even cracked an earnest smile. A successful morning had done wonders for my mood.

He'd blown out a heavy breath and clamped down on my upper arm, nodding toward the crowd. "We're meeting some friends."

"Of yours?"

His fingers were really cutting into my arm but no matter how hard I tugged he wasn't letting go. "No, yours."

I'd gone numb with shock as Jim dragged me into a small empty field behind some buildings and told me how he'd followed me all the way from Buckshot, how he'd decided that letting me run loose was fun, and how he'd tortured Will with text messages to his brother.

"He won't come," I choked out.

"Yes, he will." Jim gave me a chilly, confident smile that made me shiver.

"How can you be so sure?" If I was Will, I wouldn't come after me. Not after I'd left him standing there.

"You might not mean anything to him, but my employer does. Will wants his name, so he'll be here."

"Maybe he already found your employer," I said, my voice shaking more than I liked. "Maybe he already killed him."

"He's still very alive, and I intend to see he stays that way. Now, come on." He started walking again, dragging me back toward the crowd.

No way in hell was my life going to end like this, but trying to get away now wouldn't do me any good. I'd wait. Be patient.

"You can't kill us in public." I glanced up at him.

"Wanna bet?" He laughed and leaned over so only I could hear him. "I can kill Will Collier and disappear before anyone knows he's dead."

"What about me?"

His eyes raked over me in a way that made my skin crawl, and made me angry. "I'm gonna keep you around a while."

Like hell!

Once we reached a particularly crowded spot, I stumbled on purpose, then stomped on his foot as hard as I could. His grip on my arm loosened just enough for me to pull free and jab him in the ribs with my elbow.

Then I ran like hell, the words, "Jim had shot at us, and Jim was our hunter," playing over and over again in my head. I'd sat with him, talked to him . . . *let him pet my dog!*

"Sabrina, wait up!"

I didn't bother checking behind me. His voice sounded dangerously close, and I increased my pace accordingly, breaking into a fast trot as I searching the passing buildings for a place to hide.

Thank God for the thick Saturday afternoon crowd.

I darted into the turret connected to a store and raced up the stairs. My legs throbbed and burned with every step. Struggling for air now, I collapsed in the balcony. I could barely hear over the sound of my heavy breathing and my heart pounding, but Jim knew how to make his presence known.

"Sabrina-a-a-a-a!"

Shit! He was already at the bottom of the stairs. Groaning, I sagged against the wall, then forced my shaky legs up and peeked over the balcony.

It was too far to jump. I'd probably break a leg or worse. Down below people wandered by drinking and laughing and eating those fucking turkey legs. Calling for help didn't seem wise. I didn't want to have someone's death on my conscience—not that it would matter if I was dead. Just then I spotted Will's brother. The one who'd come to visit us at the cabin. *Sweet Jesus.* Too bad I didn't know his name.

"Get Will," I shouted at the top of my lungs.

Jim laughed while the other man's head snapped up. We made brief eye contact, then I took off up the stairs again. All I had to do was hold Jim off for a few more minutes. Help was on the way. Will had come, even if he probably hadn't come for me.

By the time I hit the roof, my legs were done, jelly and toast. I slid on the gravel, ripping my skirt and skinning my knee. It hurt like hellfire but not as bad as my legs did. Expecting a kick or a yank of my hair any second now, I did a sort of crabwalk across the roof, more gravel cutting into the palms of my hands. My legs were all tangled in my skirt, slowing me down more.

It was quieter up here away from the crowds, and there was no mistaking the sound of Jim's booted footsteps. I turned and forced myself to my feet. I might die but not on my back and *not* without a fight.

"Sabrina."

"They're coming, you know," I panted, pushing my hair off my face.

"Good. I'll kill them, too." He pulled out a long, deadly looking gun and pointed it at me. "And then, I'll be famous."

"You'll never get out of here. Once you fire that gun—"

He shrugged and waggled it back and forth. "Silencer."

"They won't let you get away."

He raised the gun, and I grabbed his wrist with both hands, pushing it upward. Out of nowhere one of Jim's huge fists connected with my jaw. I lost my grip as pain blossomed across my face, and I went down. All I could see were stars. My hand curled around some of the gravel as Jim moved closer. I forced myself to breathe, forced my vision to clear as best I could, and drew up my knees, ready to defend myself.

Jim bent over, his lips curved into a pleased smile, and pointed the gun at my forehead. "Say goodnight, Gracie."

I threw the gravel in his eyes, blinking and sputtering as some of it blew back into my face, and shoved my foot into his crotch with all my might. He fell, half on top of me, and I grabbed the gun. The muscles in my arms screamed in protest as I struggled to shove it away from me.

"Fucking bitch." Jim planted one meaty arm in the middle of my chest, bearing down with all his weight while we struggled over the gun. "Shoulda killed you last night."

"Yeah, you should have."

17

Will turned at the sound of his name. The sight of Sabrina at the top of the mini-castle sent a jolt through him just as Wynn shouted for him. Heart in his throat, Will broke into a run. He passed Wynn, whose question about John's whereabouts was lost on him.

John would just have to catch up.

Will sprinted up the narrow staircase. He hit the top step just as a loud pop echoed in his ears. He knew that sound, knew it well, and his blood ran cold. Sabrina lay pinned under a man, neither of them moving.

His feet felt as if they were stuck in swamp mud. He swallowed the lump in his throat, then forced his lungs to expand and contract.

Wynn darted past him, and pulled the man off Sabrina. "She's alive."

Sick with relief, Will moved forward on much more cooperative legs. He crossed to where Sabrina lay and sank down beside her. There was blood. A lot of it. And he still wasn't a hundred percent positive it wasn't hers.

He pushed her hair off her face and felt for a pulse, needing some form of quick reassurance. He relaxed the tiniest bit at the steady knock of her blood flowing beneath his fingers. Then he patted her down, and lifted up her shirt. His fingers came away sticky and red but luckily, there were no oozing bullet holes that he could find. "Sabrina... *Bree.*" He patted her cheek, almost smiling when her eyelashes moved.

"He's alive," Wynn said.

"I don't care." All he cared about was that Sabrina was alive.

"He needs medical attention, Will."

"Fuck *him.*" Will glanced at the man, starting slightly in surprise. The man from the bar. The one who'd raised his beer to Will the night he'd been hunting Derek Frost. "Let him bleed to death."

"Dre will just send someone else," John said from behind them.

Will turned a sharp eye in his brother's direction. "I'll take care of Dre." He nodded toward the unconscious man. "You take care of *him.*"

"His name's Jim," Sabrina hoarsely whispered, then licked her lips.

"Pat him down," Will instructed Wynn.

Wynn picked up the gun and handed it to John, who quickly made it disappear.

Sabrina struggled to sit up, one hand pressed to her jaw. "Damnit!"

"You scared the shit out of me." Even to his own ears, it sounded lame. What he really wanted to do was give her a hard shake for running off like she had. Instead, he tucked some curls behind her ear, but her wide-eyed gaze was on Jim as she scooted closer to Will.

"Guess I should have listened to you."

"Yeah, but I'll save the 'I told you so's for later," Will said.

"Is he . . . ?" She shuddered the tiniest bit.

"No," Will sighed. "He'll probably live to run away."

"Like hell. I plan to make sure he's dead by sundown," John said.

Sabrina shivered again and glanced up at Will. Her lips moved, but no words came out.

"How are we going to get him out of here?" Wynn asked.

"You're not," a big baritone voice boomed from the stairs.

Will jerked around, reaching for his gun in one fluid movement. A party of two dressed in jeans and special fair T-shirts stood at the top of the stairs. One of them had a turkey leg clasped in his hand, the other man held a gun.

"Jim, what the hell are you doing here?" Will eased to his feet and put his gun away as everything fell into place.

The man on the ground wasn't *really* named Jim, but whoever he was, he had connections. Had to if Jimmy Page was here. The Pages and Colliers didn't exactly run in the same circles, but you'd have to be deaf, dumb, and dead to not know who Jimmy Page was.

Not to mention dead if you called him Jimmy to his face.

"We're here for him."

"Like hell!" John started across the roof, but Wynn snagged a piece of his shirt, pulling him back just enough to clamp a hand down on his shoulder.

"You can't have him," Will said.

"I'm afraid it's out of my hands." Jim gave him an icy smile that said there was no room for argument.

"He hunted me. He shot at me. He tried to kill me."

"And he'll be punished, but he's family."

"I don't care if he's made—" John sputtered.

"Not *made*. Family. Mark's mom is Dad's cousin." Jim

shrugged as if to say, "What are you gonna do?" and continued, "I'm sure none of us wants to involve our families any more than we have to."

Sadly, he was right.

If they didn't let Jim have Mark, or whoever that was lying on the ground, his dad would make waves. And Big Tom Page wasn't a man you wanted to piss off. On top of which, waves meant *their* dad would find out about all of this—though the chances of him never finding out were now pretty slim.

Will nodded and reluctantly stepped out of the way. "If he ever comes after me again—"

"He won't. You have my word." Jim nodded, and the other man moved around him to where Jim's cousin lay.

"I'm holding you to that," Will added.

"Will," Sabrina said.

He turned to find her standing on shaky legs. He reached for her, wrapping an arm around her waist. "It's all right."

"He needs a doctor." The other man glanced up at Jim.

"It was an accident." Sabrina swallowed and raised her chin a notch, her eyes on their guests. "Jim hit me. He—"

"Mark," Jimmy corrected, his eyes softening slightly as he answered Sabrina. "His name's Mark."

"She didn't mean to shoot him," Will added, pulling her closer. The last thing he wanted was for Sabrina to end up in more trouble.

"Get out of here," the real Jim said with a nod of understanding. "We'll clean this up."

They were halfway down the stairs when Sabrina stopped and looked up at Will. Fear had turned her eyes more brown than green, and she still hadn't stopped shaking. "My shirt. I can't go out there like this."

"I'll go find something for her," Wynn offered, slipping past them and disappearing from view.

John followed Wynn down the stairs. "I still think we should have killed him."

"Damnit, not now, John," Will said, tightening his grip on Sabrina. "Why don't you go pack up Sabrina's stuff? Meet us back here in ten."

"How the hell am I supposed to find her stuff?" John groused.

"Five minutes that way." Sabrina pointed him in the right direction. Her arm quaked. "Look for the dog."

"Dog?"

"Yeah." Will nodded and gave him a shove in the right direction. "His name is Scamp." Once he was gone, Will turned to Sabrina. "Pull it together."

She nodded shakily, curls bobbing and eyes on the ground. "I'm sorry."

"Not nearly as sorry as I am."

18

Putting on a happy face was out of the question; I'd have to be satisfied with acting as normal as possible.

I took comfort in the feel of Will's arm around my waist as he led me out of the fair and toward my van. I kept waiting for Will to yell at me or shake me or give me that promised "I told you so," but it never came. He just tucked me into the passenger side of the van and slammed the door. He stood outside, his back to me and waited with arms crossed over his chest until John, who was, incredibly enough, a scarier version of Will, showed up with Scamp and my stuff. Despite my earlier trauma, I almost laughed at the appalled look on John's face as he handed Scamp over to Will.

We made it out of the fair without any more problems, and without a word said between us. Will followed Wynn's BMW to a Holiday Inn. The parking lot was the shiny black that only came from new asphalt and never lasted long. It was a sharp contrast to the pale pink faux stucco of the building.

"Wait here." Will opened and slammed the driver's door, briefly letting in the sound of traffic from the nearby highway.

From behind me came the sound of Scamp sighing. Finally, Will returned for us, leading me upstairs and into a chilly hotel room. I curled up on the bed, my dog clutched in my arms. "I should have listened to you."

He gave me a long, solemn stare that scared me more than anything he could have said. "Go take a shower. You smell like blood."

Flinching, I grabbed my things and stepped into the bathroom, where I closed the door, turned the shower on, and promptly threw up. After washing up, I stood under the spray until the shaking stopped. I didn't want to get out. I didn't want to face Will.

Was it possible to shower yourself to death?

Finally, I eased out and toweled off. I slipped into my tattered pink robe and wrapped another towel around my head, then took a deep breath and twisted the doorknob.

The room was empty. Even Scamp was gone. Tears pricked my eyes, and I sagged against the door frame.

Swallowing the lump in my throat, I stretched out on the bed, thinking I'd never sleep again, but I did.

When I woke up, Will was there with my dog and some food.

I sat up and pushed the towel off my head. "I'm sorry you didn't get to kill him."

"I'm sorry I dragged you into this mess." He didn't even turn at the sound of me moving around. "Come eat."

The thought of food made me want to run for the bathroom. "I'm not hungry."

"You need to eat, Sabrina."

I swung my legs over the side of the bed, trying to shake the fuzzies out of my head. "You gonna yell at me now?"

"What do you want me to say?" Will finally turned around, a scowl firmly in place as he stalked across the room. "This is why I dragged you out to the middle of nowhere! This . . . *this* is what I tried to prevent!" He stopped in front of me and grasped my chin, forcing me to look at him. His grip was firm but not painful. "Do you have any idea how many people you could have gotten hurt or, worse, killed today?"

I'd never even considered it, hadn't really had time, and words failed me. All I could muster up was a shrug and a nod.

"Not to mention what could have happened to you," he said. His tone was softer but that scowl was still firmly in place. "I should have left you on the side of the road."

I licked my lips. "What happens now?"

The flush of anger left his cheeks and his expression hardened. "Stoic man" was back. "You're safe."

"What about the guy"—here I paused to lick my lips—"who wants you dead?" I practically had to force the words out.

"He'll definitely send someone else. Or try to." *If Will didn't get to him first.*

A shiver raced through me; I hugged myself and focused on Scamp, who lay on the other queen bed watching us. "When can I go back to the fair?"

His hand fell to his side and the sound of his sigh filled my ears.

"I have to work," I explained, lamely.

"How the hell can you think about going back to work already?" He shouted loud enough to make me cringe. Loud enough that our neighbors turned the TV down. "You nearly died today, Sabrina!"

"I have to work, Will. I-I have to—" I shrank back, struggling against my tears. "I don't know what else—"

"I—" He ran a hand through his hair and turned away. "In the morning then."

I didn't know what else to do. I *had* to work.

I forced myself to choke down half a chicken leg, then

stretched out again, thankful for whatever escape I could get. When I woke up next, Will and his brother John sat at the little worktable illuminated by a sixty-watt bulb.

"Sure you don't mind taggin' along?" Will's voice was low and gruff.

"Huh. It's my pleasure," John practically growled. "Hell, I'll do it for ya."

"I need to do this."

Through sheer will, I kept my breathing steady while I listened to them plan the end for someone named Dre.

"So what about after?" John asked. "You still planning on quitting?"

"It's not quitting," Will softly said. "I'm retiring."

Somehow, that thought didn't make me feel any better. Lying still finally got to me, and I shifted, turning my back to them and sighing. Hopefully, they'd think I slept though their little conversation.

"And yeah, I'm done. This one was a little too close to home."

"Don't be such a puss. What are the odds?"

"And who the fuck knew Dre Anderson was such a dumbass?" Will added with a painful-sounding laugh. "I don't care. It's Nevis for me . . . after this."

"What about her?" John asked.

I was the only "her" involved. Stood to reason he was referring to me.

Will stayed quiet for so long I wondered if somehow I'd missed his reply. "What about her?" he echoed.

"You planning on taking her to Nevis with you?"

This time Will's answer must have been nonverbal, or so soft I just didn't hear him. Shortly after, footsteps whispered on the carpet, the door opened and closed, and John was gone.

The room fell into darkness as Will flicked the light off, then the petrified slab that doubled as a queen-sized mattress sagged the tiniest bit as he slipped into bed beside me. He touched my hair, his fingers gentle so they didn't snag in tangled curls. His finger traced the curve of my shoulder, then slipped under the covers while his breath gently moved my hair. A part of me wanted to make him stop. I wasn't sure this was a memory I wanted to carry around. Knowing I was leaving in the morning hurt even worse than losing Ronnie, but as Will nuzzled my hair, as his mouth found my neck, I didn't have the heart or the strength to say no.

I rolled over, trying to act sleepylike. Will's hand skimmed my hip, then he pulled my nightgown up. He lightly traced the inside of my thigh with those long, skillful fingers of his, and pressed his lips to my shoulder. I tugged the top of my gown downward and drew him to me, pressing my nipple against his lips, into his open mouth. I sighed at the feel of his soft tongue caressing me and my legs fell open. Together we pushed my panties off. That's when I realized he was naked. The feel of his skin on mine was electric. I reached for his cock, ready to shimmy under the covers and give him a blow job, but he stopped me, pinning my leg down with one of his. His hand dipped between my thighs to gently stroke my pussy.

"You like that?" he whispered against my skin.

Words failed me, so I licked my lips and nodded while my hips moved in time with his fingers. My clit swelled with every stroke. He rolled onto his back, pulling me on top of him and positioning me just over his cock. I slid home with a happy whimper, letting him stretch me, fill me. Will rubbed my juices on one nipple. Then sat up, pulling it into his mouth. He sucked and bit both of my breasts while I rode him one last time. I clung to him when I came, good bye playing over and over in my head as each bittersweet wave of my orgasm hit me.

Come morning, I'd never see or smell or touch Will again.

* * *

In the murky morning light of the hotel room, Will's sleeping face seemed much more relaxed. I wiped my sweaty hand on my jeans, then leaned over to give him a gentle shake. "Will."

He stretched and groaned and stared up at me through bleary eyes. A tiny smile tickled his lips.

"I have to go. Work." I wanted to kiss his cheek, or his mouth, but considering we'd never see each other again, probably not a good idea.

Smile now gone, he nodded and sat up. "Need some money for breakfast?"

"No. I've got money." I should have taken his cash; I should have asked him if I could go to Nevis with him. "I'll be right back."

I carried my stuff downstairs to the van, my steps slow and careful on the dew-covered steps. I was three-quarters of the way down when somewhere above and behind me, a door slammed. Scamp barked. I looked up in time to see him licking Will's hand. With a shake of my head and a deep steadying breath, I crossed to where he'd parked the van.

Inside, everything was just like I'd left it, including my heart. I threw my tote in and turned to take Scamp from Will. "You didn't have to bring him down."

"Saved you the extra trip." He gave me what seemed like a wistful smile. Or maybe he was still sleepy. "I filled your van up, too."

"Thanks." I reached for Scamp, jumping as Will's lips brushed my cheek.

"You could come with me."

I shook my head, reluctantly. "I'm sorry." Retirement or no, the fact remained that Will Collier killed people for a living. I just couldn't reconcile myself to that kind of life. Even though a part of my brain was screaming, "I should have said yes."

19

Will headed upstairs, pausing at the sight of Wynn waiting outside the door of his hotel room, fresh coffee in hand.

Will accepted the cup with a grunt of thanks, then slid his keycard into the door. Downstairs, the van roared to life. He kept his back to the parking lot. The sight of her leaving hurt, especially after he'd come so close to losing her yesterday. "You're up early."

"So's she." Wynn nodded toward the parking lot.

Unwilling to listen to Bree drive away, Will pushed past his brother and inside his hotel room. They'd dodged more than one bullet in the last twenty-four hours. The important thing was that Sabrina was safe. And Lord help him, he was *almost* glad she'd turned him down. He didn't know if his heart could take going through something like that again.

Wynn closed the door, then took a seat, his eyes sharp over the rim of his cup. "Why'd you let her go?"

"She actually said she was sorry I didn't get to kill Mark."

Wynn chuckled into his cup. "Sounds like something Julie might say. *Now*, why'd you let her go?"

"It's what she wanted."

"You don't *really* believe—"

"You know, Tilly hated me." He absently peeked out the curtain to watch the traffic on the nearby highway hurtle past—and reassure himself that Sabrina's van was gone. "She even said so. Bree said it, too; more than once." He laughed harshly.

"But Tilly hated you for different reasons."

"And Bree hates me for all the right ones." He shrugged, "Or she wouldn't have left."

"What are those reasons?"

"I kill people for a living." He might have lied but he'd never made excuses or apologies for his job. But now, he definitely had regrets.

"And?"

"And? *And?* What the hell else is there? Oh yeah, I kidnapped her, and I nearly got her killed."

Wynn set his cup on the table. "I could argue that she nearly got herself killed. She did leave you after all."

"She would have never been in any danger if I . . ."

"If you what?"

"If I hadn't tried to return her journals, if I hadn't bought her that van. If I . . ." Will shook his head.

"Finish it, Will."

"If I'd left her standing on the side of the road."

"If you'd left her there, she might be dead anyway."

"Point taken, but still . . ."

"But still what? You love her, go after her. Tell her."

"I never said I loved her."

"You didn't have to. So, you're really through?"

Nodding, he sank onto the unmade bed, feeling all of his almost forty years. "Yeah, I'm done."

"Just gonna go off to Nevis all by yourself."

"That's the plan. Soon as we take care of Dre Anderson."

"You know I can't be involved."

" 'Cause Julie would kill you," Will said with a nod.

"I'll be there in spirit." They clinked coffee cups.

Once Wynn was gone, Will packed up his stuff. It didn't take long. And as soon as John got his ass up and moving, they were heading to Phoenix.

"I don't like this," Will said, thinking of Sabrina. "We're not ready." He wished there was another way to take care of Dre Anderson. Sadly, there wasn't.

They'd made the drive to Phoenix in record time and now sat outside the six-story glass-and-steel building that held the investment firm of Anderson-Frost. They could have flown, but guns didn't mix with airport security and they were in a hurry, which made buying one in Phoenix out of the question.

"We're as ready as we'll ever be," John said from the passenger seat.

They'd spent only twenty-four hours tracking Dre Anderson's movements. Not enough time to get a feel for him or know who'd miss him once he was dead. Or even how long after his death before anyone realized he was gone. But as soon as Dre found out that Mark Green was no longer in play, he'd hire someone else.

It was almost twilight when Dre's Audi exited the underground parking garage, and they followed him all the way back to his house. After assuring themselves that Dre was alone and safely tucked in for the night, they waited. At 3:00 AM they went back, ski masks firmly in place, and Will waited impatiently while John disabled Dre's alarm.

The sliding glass door opened effortlessly, Dre assured of his safety by the alarm that should have beeped but didn't. The house was quiet and smelled faintly of sandalwood. On soft-soled shoes they made their way through the lower level, too intent on the job to bother with checking out their surroundings. Upstairs, they paused long enough to check each door along the hallway until they found the right one.

No more than a minute or three had passed since they entered the house, but it seemed like a lifetime to Will. He took a deep breath and slowly, softly exhaled before following John into Dre's bedroom. He couldn't remember the last time he'd been so nervous about a job.

They'd agreed during the drive that John would be the triggerman. For that reason he let John take the lead. They had no intention of waking Dre and having a confrontation. It just wasn't necessary. And if Dre knew his man had been caught and injured, then he also knew they were onto him. If his snores were anything to go by, he wasn't worried, though.

Will stood at the foot of the king-sized bed while John moved closer. He leveled the gun a few short inches from Dre's head and glanced at Will, who gave a slight nod. John pulled the trigger with no hesitation, then shot him again in the heart.

Dre Anderson was an arrogant, stupid man and had just paid the price for his arrogance, in spades.

"Let's get out of here," Will murmured.

20

Two weeks had passed since I'd left Will at the Holiday Inn on I-35. I'd managed to find a second job and a cheap efficiency that rented by the month. Between waitressing in the greasy spoon and working the fair every weekend, I'd fallen into bed every night too exhausted to think about Will. Okay, well, almost too exhausted.

It was a muggy, late-summer, Saturday afternoon, the kind the South is famous for. The cards had started to stick to my fingers as I shuffled, and both Scamp and I had missed lunch.

I was all ready to take a break when a pretty brunette strolled up, a hopeful smile on her face. "Mind if I sit down?"

"Help yourself." Inwardly, I groaned. "I'm just going to grab some water." I retrieved a bottle from the cooler under the table, cracked the lid, and poured half into Scamp's dish.

"He's a cutie," she said.

"Thanks." I smiled and took a few seconds to study her. She looked as if the heat didn't bother her, despite wearing jeans.

"It's forty dollars, cash only." I discretely wiped my hands on my skirt, then shuffled the cards as she slipped two twenties onto the table. After tucking the money away in my box, I said, "Anything in particular you'd like to know or just a general reading?"

Her glossy lips pursed, she slid her sunglasses back on her head. "Actually, I'm worried about someone." Flawless green eyes stared back at me. "Can you do a reading for someone else?"

"I can try."

"It's my brother-in-law."

My throat went dry. I reached for the water bottle and took a tiny sip. "Go on."

"He's leaving . . . he's going away." Sighing, she leaned forward, crossing her arms in front of her. "I just want to know if maybe he'll find someone special. I hate to think of him down there in Nevis with nothing but the fish for company."

The half-shuffled cards fell to the table. Echoing her own sigh, I stacked them up, searching for an appropriate response. There was no doubt in my mind she was talking about Will. "I don't think I can help you."

"I disagree. I think you can. I also think you just don't want to."

Lips pursed, I slipped her money out and slid it across the table toward her. "No."

She shook her head. "I'm not leaving until you agree to see Will one last time."

"No."

"And I can be damn stubborn. Just ask Wynn."

"I don't intend to ask Wynn anything."

"Will's miserable." She waved a hand. "Oh, he tries to hide it, but you can tell."

"He'll recover." Just like I would. Though knowing he was unhappy sure didn't help. I sucked in some air, hoping to relieve the ache in my chest.

"What's the problem? He loves you; I'm assuming you love him." She stared at me for a few heartbeats as if waiting for me to fill in the blanks.

"He kills people for a living."

"He's retired."

"That doesn't negate what he did."

"Would it make you feel any better if—"

"No."

"Let me finish." Her face hardened slightly in anger. "If I said I had the same hangups about Wynn's job? I'm not blind and I'm not an idealist. I do understand how you feel but . . . Will's done. He's retiring. He's *getting out*."

"How do you get past . . . it all?" I asked.

"I don't ask questions I don't want answers to. And I pray every time he leaves on a job. It is what it is. You can't change what the Collier men are, but their occupations don't make them bad husbands, bad brothers, bad sons, or even bad men. Take Wynn, for instance. He never hurt anyone who didn't deserve it. And despite his job, I wouldn't trade him for anything," she said with a chuckle. "At least you'll know where Will is every night."

"I don't know." I could feel myself wavering, though. A part of me wanted to say yes and just ride off into the sunset with Will. "What if he gets bored?"

"I'm sure you can find ways to keep him busy." She gave me a naughty grin that I couldn't help but return. "Just . . . think about it. Will leaves on Wednesday. We're throwing a going-away party for him Tuesday night at our house." She slid a business card toward me. "And he won't be home again until Thanksgiving."

Nodding, I slid my fingers over the edge of the card.

"See ya." She left, quickly disappearing into the thick crowd. That's when I realized I hadn't even asked her name. The card read WYNN AND JULIE COLLIER and had their address and phone number listed, and 7:00 was scrawled on the corner in blue pen.

I thought about it all day and into the following week, trying to rationalize what going to Nevis meant. Hell, trying to rationalize what going to Wynn and Julie's meant. What if Will didn't really miss me? What if he didn't *really* want me there? What if by showing up, I just made things stupid and awkward for his family?

I'd even contemplated calling Julie to talk some more, but never managed to work up the nerve. By the time the sun broke through the curtains Tuesday morning, I was exhausted from another restless night but my reservations didn't stop me from packing. The drive to Dallas would take right around five hours.

I glanced down at Scamp in his doggy bed. "What do you think, dude?"

He stared up at me, one eyebrow quirked, stood and shook, as if to say, "You know me. I'm game for whatever."

Groaning, I stretched. Going to Will went against everything I believed in. But he had taken care of me, and I knew deep down inside that he cared for me. Maybe even loved me. Just like I knew I'd missed him terribly the last couple of weeks.

With one last sigh, I threw back the covers and got ready to pack.

The steering wheel was slippery under my hands as I circled Wynn and Julie's block for a third time. Four cars, none of them over two years old, and Will's Tahoe were parked out front or in the driveway. And the neighborhood was so nice, I worried one of Julie's neighbors might have my van towed. Finally, I gritted my teeth and made myself park just past the next-door neighbor's mailbox. I climbed from the van, shook the wrinkles from my best skirt, and called for Scamp. I hoped Julie and Wynn wouldn't mind, but it was too hot to leave him alone in the van. And besides, if it was a problem, I had an excuse to leave. Even after doing two readings for myself, which I normally *never* do, I still wasn't convinced this was the right move. But I'd decided to play it by ear.

Scamp licked my hand, a signal to get my ass in gear. I slammed the van's door and clipped his leash on him. We quickly walked past a black Lexus and a sporty red BMW convertible. I was so out of my league, but I forced my feet to keep moving as I stepped onto the grass and crossed to the walkway. I never even got to ring the bell as the door flew open and Julie stepped outside.

"Good. You made it." She reached out and scratched Scamp under the chin.

"I hope it's okay," I said, giving him a jiggle.

"It's fine. But Bud, that's Will's dad, brought his cat." She motioned me inside. "He doesn't go anywhere without that little fucker."

I snorted, and tried not to let my surroundings intimidate me. Julie was nice, Wynn had seemed nice, from what little I knew. How bad could the rest of them be?

"Come on. Everyone's outside where the lord and master is wowing us with his fantabulous grilling skills."

I followed her down the hall and into a bright, sunny kitchen that would make a gourmet chef envious. That's when it hit me. It had been years since I'd cooked in a real kitchen or kept a real house. What if I didn't remember how? I stopped dead in my tracks while Julie continued on to the back door. "I can't cook."

Laughing softly, Julie turned and leaned against the back door.

"I can heat stuff up," I explained lamely, "but I . . . I don't know how to . . . to be all domestic and stuff."

"Honey, I don't think he cares. Besides, Delle taught all the boys to cook. Now, come on." She yanked open the door, letting in the sound of laughter, but I still couldn't move.

"Does he know?"

"He's about to." She stood, patiently waiting until I joined her.

21

Will nearly dropped his beer at the sight of Sabrina standing in Julie's kitchen door.

"Who's that?" his sister, Dani, asked.

He dropped the hose he'd been spraying her with and glanced at Wynn, who just shrugged. His mom and dad sat under a nearby tree, talking and still unaware they had a new guest. Julie pursed her lips and quirked an eyebrow.

"Dude," Wynn murmured, "if you don't hurry up, she's gonna leave."

That got Will moving.

"The kitchen is all yours." Julie gave him an encouraging pat on the arm as she stepped past him.

He slowly climbed the porch steps and slid his sunglasses off as he stepped inside. She looked so pretty, and he didn't have a clue what to say to her. "What are you doing here?"

She shrugged, her shoulders barely lifting and falling. "Heard there was a party."

He couldn't hold back the smile that tugged at his lips. "Julie."

She nodded, shyly. "She came to see me."

Will swallowed and forced himself to ask the question that was perched toward the back of his tongue. "Did you change your mind?"

She nodded again and released a shaky sigh, as if she'd been holding her breath. "I-I don't . . ." she ended on a sniffle.

Will had finally figured out that it wasn't just his job that had her so scared. But he wasn't her mom and he wasn't Ronnie. He wasn't leaving.

Will took Scamp from her and set the dog on the floor, then wrapped his arms around her waist. "I promise you I'm not going anywhere. Not for a long, long time."

"You have to promise me something else." Sabrina swallowed hard and looked up at him, her hazel eyes clear.

"Anything."

"Never again. Promise me you will never again . . . you know. Ever!"

Smiling, he cupped her face in his hands and pressed his lips to hers. "Promise."

"I mean it."

"So do I."

HOOKED

John and Tish

1

With every step he took, John Collier's chances of ever having children shrank. Why the hell had he let his sister talk him into wearing thick support hose? Oh yeah, because shaving his legs had seemed like too high a price to pay just to kill that no good piece of shit, Mark Green.

He kept his head down as he pushed the housekeeping trolley along the hotel's hallway, his balls whimpering in protest. At Room 1416 he pulled out the keycard, opened the door, and called out in a much-practiced falsetto, "Housekeeping?"

No answer.

Water was running, and the sharp crisp scent of apples and lemons made his mouth pucker slightly. His target was in the shower. He glanced over his shoulder, reassuring himself that the hallway was empty, and nearly lost his grip on the door as he fought with his long red wig. Resisting the urge to rip it off his head and throw it in the cart's trash, John grabbed his gun and shoved it into the middle of a stack of towels.

The door softly clicked closed behind him.

"Meester Green! I have towels."

"Just leave them."

John froze at the sound of a woman's voice. In the six weeks he'd been hunting Mark Green, he'd never heard a peep about a woman. Then again, Mark had never struck him as the type who was actually successful with women. "Jess, ma'am."

John set the towels on an ornately upholstered chair, pulled his gun free of the stack, and gave the suite a quick once-over. King-sized bed and pastel furnishings that coordinated with the small sitting area just inside the balcony, connecting door, girly paraphernalia scattered every-*damn*-where and . . . *Jesus!*

He jumped and a burst of adrenaline raced through him as he caught sight of his unfamiliar reflection in the dresser's mirror. He looked like a fucking drag queen (a 6'1" one, with long curly hair, subtly smoky eyes, and 44D breasts). According to his sister, Danielle, who'd spent hours teaching him the art and science of makeup application, he made a damn *fine* drag queen. She'd laughed so hard, she'd nearly busted a seam. He still wasn't sure he'd ever speak to her again.

Now, who was the woman, and where the hell was Mark Green?

John turned away from his reflection and adjusted the bra strap riding up his back, resigned to waiting. He threw the door's security lock into place and crossed the room to where her suitcase was flopped open on the bed. With a quick glance at the bathroom door, he shoved his hand in and dug around until his hand closed on what he was looking for. Pantyhose.

John positioned himself outside the bathroom as the water stopped. The seconds slowly ticked off as he waited for the woman to join him. He held his gun firmly in one hand and the pantyhose in the other.

She stepped out of the bathroom with one towel wrapped around her head and another around her tiny, lithe body.

John lifted his gun and pointed it at the back of her head. "Don't move."

She froze, then spun around, one hand in the air, one clutching her towel. Funny, the brief hint of fear disappeared as her expressive blue eyes widened and her face did a weird twitching thing. It was his disguise. Shit!

Her lips quivered and then a tiny snort of laughter escaped. She pointed toward her suitcase. "Take my clothes. Please, help yourself."

"Very funny." She'd obviously seen right past his wig and makeup, which hadn't been meant for fooling more than the casual observer. John could feel his face burning under all the makeup he wore.

"No, really." Her face turned red and her lips continued to twitch at her obvious struggle to contain her laughter. "Knock yourself out."

"You're not my size," he said, deadpan. How the hell was he supposed to get information out of her when he was dressed like this? "Now sit." He motioned toward the bed with the gun, pleased when she moved. He had no intention of shooting her.

She sniffed, her lips still twitching. "You don't want to do this."

"Where's Mark?" He clamped a hand down on her shoulder, refusing to let himself be distracted by her soft, warm skin. An erection while wearing hosiery just might kill him.

"Playing poker. He won't be back for hours." She primly crossed her legs and looked up at him.

He grabbed her hands and secured them behind her back with the pantyhose. "I don't want to hurt you, so sit still and don't scream."

"Sure, fine, but do you know who I am?"

"Don't care." He pulled the hosiery tight, satisfied with his handiwork.

"You will." Water leaked from underneath the towel that covered her hair and trickled down her neck, and her towel was slowly working its way loose.

He laughed softly, doubting the tiny woman in front of him had anything that could hurt him—beyond her body. "Why's that?"

"I'm Tish Page, you dumbass."

"Hell." And fuck and a whole string of curse words ran through his head loudly enough to bust his eardrums while the rest of him was numb with shock. "*The* Tish Page?" he finally managed to work out.

"Yup."

"Big Tom's daughter?"

"Yup."

"Fuck." John sank into the bed, his shoulders slumped. He now had a much bigger problem than impending sterility. "How do you know Mark Green? You his—"

"*Cousin.*" The stern, exasperated expression on her delicate face spoke volumes. "What do you want with Mark?"

"You didn't hear? He tried to kill my brother." He shrugged and arched an eyebrow. "Is this going to be a problem for you?"

"Don't be a dumbass. Of course it is!"

"*Mark,*" John prompted with bravado he didn't feel. Tying up Tish Page was the dumbest thing he'd ever done.

"He's also my bodyguard," Tish sighed. "And if you kill him, my dad will be pissed."

John groaned. After Big Tom had found out about Mark trying to make a name for himself by taking out one of the Colliers, he'd laid down the law, stating it was family business and he would handle it. John had decided it was also Collier family business and hunted Mark down on his own. "So guarding you is Mark's punishment for trying to kill my brother."

Her cheeks turned pink, and she made a choking gurgling sound. Anger probably. He tended to do that to women.

"Could you untie me, please?" She swallowed hard and tried to move her hands, loosening the towel in the process. A little bit more and she'd be exposed. "This really hurts."

John decided he'd rather risk her escaping than her embarrassment (and anger) if she did lose that towel. He reached for her wrists and quickly undid the knot. He tossed the hosiery aside and stood in front of her. "So this room is in Mark's name . . ."

"For my security. The family's been getting threats. You know how it is." Her lush lips curved into a smile, and that was the point where the enormity of what he'd done hit him.

John was sitting with the half-naked daughter of one of the biggest connected families south of the Mason-Dixon. "I'm so fucked."

"Nice outfit, by the way. You make a great maid."

He reached up and pulled off the wig, clutching it in his free hand. "You know I have to kill him."

"You *can't*."

"He tried—"

"You men, I swear!" She stood up and crossed her arm over her generous breasts. "You're all so stupid and pigheaded. If women ran things—"

"If women ran things, all our guns would be pink." Jesus! What a pain in the ass! He wasn't sure she was worth the trouble he'd get into if his dad found out where he was and what he'd nearly done . . . whose room he was in and who he'd tied up, not to mention the whole "in drag" thing. "When's Mark due back from the casino?"

"Hell if I know!"

"You said earlier he'd be gone a while."

"I lied! He's supposed to escort me to a party this evening, so he's got to come back soon."

"Get dressed."

Her upper lip curled the slightest bit. "I'm not dressing in front of you."

"Then go in the bathroom." John stalked across the room and tried the handle to the connecting door. "How do I get in?"

"Keycard," she drawled sarcastically.

He could literally feel her eyes rolling as she spoke. He slipped the keycard from the pocket of his maid's uniform and stuck it into the lock.

"Anyone ever tell you what great legs you have?"

"My sister."

Tish laughed, then said in a deadly serious tone, "Don't turn around until I'm dressed."

"I wouldn't think of it."

While Tish dressed, John searched Mark's room. It was a disappointingly short venture. The room was laid out exactly like Tish's, but neater. The closet held a tux that looked rented. In the bathroom there was a shaving kit, cologne, and a toothbrush in an orderly fashion. Mark's suitcase held dark slacks and half a dozen dress shirts he hadn't bothered to hang up. And no weapons. Not a very effective bodyguard!

Mark Green was a wannabe thug, hoping to follow in the footsteps of his (in)famous cousins, to carve out a place in the family business. Which was the only reason John could figure he'd gone after Will. What a dumbass.

"Find anything interesting?"

"Can I turn around now?" John countered, surprised he hadn't heard her approach.

"Yeah," she said dryly.

John turned and once again caught his unfamiliar reflection

in the dresser mirror. Tish laughed from her spot against the doorjamb. She now wore snug sweatpants and a white shirt that stopped just above her belly button and showed off her tan. Her long wet hair hung in straight dark hanks, framing the face of the prettiest devil he'd ever seen. She had creamy skin, a tiny straight nose, and thin eyebrows arched over those gorgeous eyes. A curvy, expressive mouth completed the picture.

He had to get out of here, and soon.

"Are you done?"

"Sorry." Thank God his makeup hid any telltale blush.

"How did you know we were here?"

"I did my homework." Unfortunately, he hadn't done it very well. He'd been in too much of a rush to catch Mark before he went to ground again, or he would have known about Tish. "How long has he been down there?"

"Since we got in this morning." She rolled her eyes and turned toward her own room. "He should be back soon. The bridesmaids' tea starts in just over an hour."

He studied her for a few heartbeats. "I'm guessing you're not the blushing bride?" John said, following her.

"No." Turning, she propped her hands on her hips and tilted her head to the side.

"Good. Go get Mark . . . Please." All this waiting was making him edgy, and his face itched under the makeup.

"I have to get ready for tonight, and you know—" She turned and jabbed him in the chest. He was saved from any serious damage thanks to all the padding that filled out his bra. "He might not be worth his daddy's sperm, but he's still my cousin. I'm *not* going to help you kill him."

John stayed silent, his eyes fixed on that long pink fingernail.

"And if you kill him, I don't have a bodyguard."

He opened his mouth to ask a question but had to wait as

Tish dove for the bed where she'd tossed her buzzing cell phone.

"Yeah . . . uh huh . . ." She glanced at John, and he narrowed his eyes. "No! You *can't*. You piece of shit!" She held the phone to her mouth and screamed, "Fucker!" Then she threw the phone on the bed and turned her narrow-eyed gaze on John. "He knows you're here."

John reached for his gun, only to realize he'd left it on Tish's dresser and she stood between him and it. "Where is he?"

"In a taxi on the way to the airport, Jiminy Frickin' Cricket! I hope you're happy!"

That would be putting it mildly. He blew out a resigned breath and made to push past Tish so he could retrieve his gun, only to stop short at the sound of her voice.

"Where the hell are *you* going?" She raised her chin a notch and crossed her arms over her ample chest.

He turned and retrieved his wig, cramming it on his head. "The airport." He fussed with it, digging the extra curls out of the netting.

"Like hell!"

John tugged the wig into place, then moved to check his appearance in the mirror. "Like hell nothing. How did he even know I was here?"

Tish reached up and snatched off the wig, jerking his head in the process. "He'll be on a plane by the time you get to the airport."

John grabbed for his wig and missed, cursing under his breath. No way could he walk out of this room without it. "I'll find him."

"Not today, Super Cop." Looking smug, she tucked the wig behind her back.

John slowly closed the space between them. "Then tomorrow. Or the day after, or the day after that. Your cousin tried to kill my brother. He deserves to be punished."

Tish danced back a few steps. "Not today, not tomorrow, not the next day, or the day after that."

John frowned down at her, suddenly wondering if he was missing something.

"You ran off my bodyguard." She propped her hands on her hips, his wig dangling from her fingers.

"Sorry?" he offered up lamely. He wanted the wig and wanted away from her.

"Sorry, my ass! *You're* going to take his place."

"*What?*"

She gave him a deadpan look that made his insides shrivel. "Or I call my dad."

"I have to—"

She snatched her cell phone off the bed and wiggled it at him, a sly grin on her face.

"You're shitting me." His shoulders slumped. She had him. She knew it, and so did he.

"Never would I shit you," she drawled. And she looked serious, too.

He had to give it one last try. "I *really* need—"

"I'll do it. I bet Daddy will be thrilled to know you're still after Mark."

Not near as thrilled as John's dad. The only reason Mark was still alive was because Tish's brother, Jim, had stepped in and saved his sorry ass before John could finish the job.

"Aren't you a little old for a bodyguard?"

"No!" Her brows drew together slightly as she morphed from indignant to concerned in seconds. "How old do I look?"

"Old . . . enough." *Please drop it please God let her drop it.*

"*How* old?"

"Old . . . e-enough." He nodded for good measure. *Drop it, Tish. Drop it now.*

"Specifically . . ." One of her pretty little eyebrows arched.

Shit. "Twenty . . ." six, seven, and eight clicked off in his head but, "Thirty," came out of his mouth.

She gasped, her upper lip curling in horror.

"-ish," he added hopefully. "Thirty-ish."

"I'm twenty-seven, and in case you didn't get the memo, my father's a powerful man."

"I know who your father is." John nodded, wondering what the point was.

"He has enemies."

"I can imagine."

"Which is why you *are* going to take Mark's place. Uh uh—" She waggled a finger at him before he could tell her no. "I don't go *anywhere* without a bodyguard. And my best friend is getting married, so for the next four days, *you* will be my bodyguard. *Comprende?*"

"Com—" He nodded glumly. "Yeah. Just—"

"What?"

"Nothing." *Don't ask me if your ass looks fat because I won't lie.* Not that Tish's ass looked fat. She actually had a really nice heart-shaped ass that made him think things that could get him killed, but the last girl he'd shared his little "no lying" problem with had tortured him with questions about her ass, her clothes, her friends, her job, anything she could think of . . . then dumped him after the fun had worn off.

"Well, what are you waiting for?" She held his wig out to him, letting it dangle from her fingertips. "Go get your stuff."

He snatched the wig from her hands, turning and using the mirror to, once again, get it on straight. "There's no reason—"

"There's every reason. And since you ran my escort off, you just became my boyfriend."

"What?" he shouted.

"You heard me." She settled her hands on her hips again. "By the way, what's your name?"

Fucked? "John . . . John Collier."

Tish couldn't hold back a chuckle once the door closed behind him. Underneath all that makeup and stuff was one *fine*-looking man. Even under the maid uniform, there was no hiding that tight ass. And those legs . . . she sighed. The hair under his tights, though. What the hell had he been thinking? Nobody in their right mind would have believed he was a woman.

Thank God Mark had gotten her text message and called.

Spending the next four days in Nassau with that fine-ass hunk of man posing as her devoted boyfriend versus four days with her loser cousin who'd bum money and whine about time away from the poker tables . . . Hmmm, not a difficult choice to make—at all.

John would never know he'd had a fast one pulled on him, and his presence at her side would definitely shut up her ex-boyfriend Vince and his stupid friends.

2

By the time Tish finished drying her hair, John had moved into Mark's room lock, stock, and wig. Instead of getting cleaned up, he sat on the bed looking incredibly dejected.

"You can't go to the tea dressed like that," she said, referring to his dress and wig. "Not that you're not cute, but my friends would never believe you were my boyfriend."

"What tea?" A frown marred his tanned forehead.

"The *bridesmaids'* tea." Didn't he pay attention? "Do you need some cold cream for that makeup?" She pointed toward her own room. "I have some really good—"

"I brought my own." He slowly stood, sad and defeated as a fat kid denied a third piece of cake.

God, the next few days were going to be a blast!

"Okay, well, lose the drag getup and get a move on. You've only got about forty-five minutes, and I hate being late."

Back in her own bathroom, Tish pulled her hair into a French twist, her mind distracted with thoughts of what John

Collier might look like out of his drag getup. Besides hot, of course.

Everyone knew the Collier men were hot. At least, that's what she'd heard.

By the time she slipped into her strappy Via Spiga slingbacks and knocked on John's door, the suspense was killing her. "Come on, Johnny Boy. Time to show and tell, sweetie pie." She bit back a giggle.

He flung the door open, and the first thing she noticed was the scowl on his face. The second, his incredibly broad shoulders.

"Hope you don't have a lot of shindigs to go to. I packed light."

After meeting him in drag, his clean-cut appearance, the type she normally associated with bankers and lawyers, made her heart pick up speed and her mouth go dry. His chocolate brown hair was parted slightly off-center and perfectly combed. He had just enough tan to set off his silvery-blue eyes, and a square jaw that blended fabulously into great cheekbones. His nose had been broken at least once and combined with that kissable mouth... Yum!

"Are you done?"

Chuckling, she met his gaze head-on. "No, but it'll do—for now."

"You sure? You're the one who said you didn't want to be late, but if you want more time to stare at me..."

Arrogant ass. She almost laughed again.

"Zip me?" She spun around, unwilling to give him a chance to tell her no.

He held the base of the zipper tight and slowly pulled upward, his fingers warm through the thin material of her dress.

She waited for him to make small talk, tell her how nice she looked, how great she smelled, *anything*. "You look great, by the way."

"Thanks. Does this room have a keycard?"

"What happened to yours?"

"I left it in the maid's cart when I returned it."

Obtuse would be putting it mildly. She sighed, glad he couldn't see her rolling her eyes. "We'll stop at the front desk."

In the elevator she found herself waiting, yet again, for John to compliment her, but he apparently worked on a completely different wavelength than the rest of Earth's men.

"So, John..."

"Yes, ma'am."

"It's Tish."

"Tish," he echoed from beside her. He stood with hands clasped behind his back, military precise.

"So John, what do you do when you're not... what exactly do you do?"

Instead of a response, he visually inspected the entire elevator, checking the upper quadrants for heaven only knew what. "Are there cameras?"

"Never mind." She knew plenty about men who couldn't talk about their work, especially in public. "What do you do when you're not working?"

"Get ready to work."

"And?" she prompted.

"And what?" He frowned slightly.

"What do you do for fun?"

"Work."

"You don't play golf or bowl or tennis or—" *fuck?*

"No."

Tish breathed a small sigh of relief as they reached the

ground floor and the elevator doors slid open. She was out of small talk and unsure how much more of Mr. Excitement she could have taken.

John hadn't missed Tish's fishing for compliments; he'd just chosen to ignore it. The last thing he wanted to do was get jammed up. And he could see himself getting *very* jammed up with her—in more ways than one. Dammit, she was hot!

He stepped out of the elevator, convinced more than ever that the next four days were going to be hell.

She dragged him across the ornate lobby to the desk, and proceeded to con the clerk out of another key. The woman behind the counter never even blinked twice, never noticed that he'd checked in under another name. He figured most people saw whatever they expected to see and not much else. A phenomenon that made his job that much easier.

Smiling, he pocketed the keycard and nodded to the woman. They were halfway across the lobby's marble floor when Tish started squealing and darted away on her dangerously high heels.

She accosted a woman, assaulting her with air kisses and more squealing that seemed to echo off the lobby's high ceilings and pierce the ears of every man in a fifty-yard radius. John caught more than one man rubbing his ear. He stood silently behind her, scanning the crowd for an imagined assailant, though he figured that Tish wasn't the one who'd need help if she was attacked. All she'd have to do was that squealy thing again and maybe pierce her attacker's heart with the heel of her shoe.

"Ohhh, hi," the redhead cooed. She leaned toward him, her arm tightly hooked through Tish's as she looked him up and down. Her dress was almost a duplicate of the one Tish wore: knee length, spaghetti straps, snug, low-cut, and silky, except Red's was a bright yellow and Tish's was light blue.

"This is Samantha." Tish blinked up at him rapid-fire, as if she were sending him a message in Morse code. Whatever... he totally missed it.

Samantha held out a hand and John reached for it, giving it a firm shake. He could tell from the disappointed expression on her face she'd expected hand kissing or some other form of homage, but he wasn't about to kiss some woman's hand when he had no idea where it had been.

"You've been holding out on me, Tish, not telling me about your new man." Samantha licked her lips and grinned, eyeing him as if he were her last meal. "I bet you know all about me."

"No." He might have to play Tish's boyfriend, but that didn't mean he had to do it her way. He ignored Tish's frantic eye and brow movements, and shrugged. "Nothing."

"Strong and silent much," Samantha scoffed and arched an eyebrow in Tish's direction.

"Okay, well"—Tish tucked her free arm in his—"Samantha's the slut of the group. And if you see her drinking tequila, head for the hills. Now you know all about her."

Both women laughed, but the deadpan expression Tish tossed his way convinced him to stay as far away as Samantha as he could humanly manage.

"He's *hot*," Samantha stage-whispered. "Does the rest of the wedding party know about him?"

"Huh uh," Tish said and kept on walking.

"Oh, my."

John didn't have time to wonder about "the rest of the wedding party" as the two ladies dragged him down a narrow hallway and into a replica of a cozy English pub.

He took in the dark interior and heavy red leather chairs. They clashed drastically with the gold and white balloons and streamers that seemed to have exploded all over what would have been an English pub. "I thought this was a tea."

Tish nudged him, and he let it go.

Four other women, all in varying shades of the same dress as hers, and a fifth in white, stood clustered around a table laughing and clutching their martini glasses.

The one in white broke away from the crowd and strode toward them, a huge smile on her perfectly made-up face. "You're late!"

Tish and Samantha's apologies were followed by more air-kisses and squealing. John was edging his way toward the bar when Tish's voice stopped him.

"This is Natasha. Our lovely bride. Isn't her ring gorgeous?"

Natasha held out her left hand for him to admire.

It was gaudy. And ugly and pretentious. It screamed, "I just sold myself for five carats and a summer house in Hilton Head," or Palm Beach or wherever the hell people like Natasha vacationed. He swallowed the lump in his throat and muttered, "If you say so."

Tish jabbed him in the side with her elbow. "John!"

"It's big." He nodded and forced his lips to curve upward into a smile. That, at least, wasn't a lie. He wondered if the ring was a reflection on the groom's lack of sexual prowess, then bit his tongue to keep from asking Natasha if that was the case.

"You didn't tell me you were bringing someone." A wide-eyed Natasha gave him a strained smile.

"I can skip the wedding," John offered.

"You didn't even tell me you were dating anyone!" Natasha's lower lip rolled out the tiniest bit as a woman who reminded John of a young Sophia Loren approached. Again, she wore a dress like Tish's but in red.

Tish swallowed hard. "I'm sorry, Nat, but you've been so busy . . ."

"I knew." The brunette gave him a calculating, flirty smile.

"Well aren't you the quiet one," Natasha said, before checking him out again. "Who knew?"

Once Natasha seemed satisfied with Tish's explanation, the women looped arms and turned their backs to him, hips wiggling in a disturbing rhythm as they crossed to where the rest of the bridesmaids waited.

Relieved over having a chance to catch his breath, John took a seat at the bar, as far away from the women as he could get, and spent three of the most miserable hours of his life perched on that barstool. By the time Tish tugged him free, he had a raging headache from the high-pitched chatter and laughter, a hell of a buzz, knew everything there was to know about the bartender's ex-wives (all three of them), and needed food.

"Wasn't that fun?" Tish gushed as they exited the bar. Not even her smile or the feel of her curvy body pressed against his as they crossed the nearly empty lobby could distract him from his growling stomach.

"No." He wanted his bed, room service, ibuprofen, and lots of peace and quiet. They stepped into the elevator and instead of punching the button for the fourteenth floor, Tish hit the 2.

"You hit the wrong button."

"No, I didn't."

"Yeah, you did." John jabbed the correct button.

The elevator stopped on two anyway, and the doors slid open.

"Come on." Tish attempted to drag him out of the elevator, but he didn't budge. "We're going to eat. Come on!"

"We're going back to the room."

Free hand propped on her hip, Tish said, "We're *going* to eat with the girls."

John stared at the hand tugging on his. "Room service.

We're ordering room service." He yanked her back into the elevator and punched the CLOSE DOOR button, thankful they were alone. He didn't let her go until they were moving again.

"You're an ass!"

He snorted, a smile tickling his lips. "Tell me something I don't already know." He held up a finger before she could speak. "And don't threaten to call your dad again. I'm here, but I am *not* your slave."

"Hummpf."

"Now, I've had a long day, I'm hungry and tired, and I want room service."

Tish crossed her arms over her chest and faced forward, her shoulders stiff. "Fine, but don't think you're getting out of spa day tomorrow."

Oh, hell no! "Spa day?"

"Yup." She rolled her shoulders as if she really, *really* needed that spa day.

"I'm not going."

"You have to. You're my bodyguard," she smugly informed him.

Maybe going after Mark Green had been a bad idea.

Tomorrow was going to suck more than today had.

Lots more. John sighed.

After a French Dip sandwich and some home fries, John stretched out in his bed with *Law and Order* reruns for company. He never slept well in hotels. At least for the first few nights, and he needed the noise to sleep. Not to mention his friend in the room next door.

She definitely qualified as ten kinds of distraction. And as much as it galled him to cater to her (almost) every whim, he didn't see where he had much choice at this point.

The air-conditioning clicked off, and he came awake with a

start. The television was now silent and black. Apparently it had been on some sort of timer. He sighed then frowned as a soft buzzing noise penetrated his consciousness. He stared at the ceiling, listening, trying to pinpoint the source of the mosquitolike sound.

It was definitely coming from Tish's room.

John threw back the covers and crossed to the connecting door, leaning closer as he tried to place the noise. Then his eyes widened and he jumped back from the door as if it was on fire. He leaned close again, then groaned.

Tish was masturbating.

3

Today was going to rock!

While an itty-bitty, teeny-weeny part of her felt bad for dragging John to the spa, the rest of Tish was tickled shitless. He was so stoic, so uptight, a part of her wanted to see just how far she could push him.

John knocked at the connecting door. "Breakfast is here."

She'd come to Nassau to watch one of her best friends get married, determined to not only have a good time but not let her ex-boyfriend *ruin* said good time. That was where John came in. And whether he liked it or not, he was going to have to play her game.

No matter how appealing it was to let her friends think she was spending all her free time doing the nasty with John, she was *not* letting some pig-headed man arm-twist her into spending the next three days holed up in her hotel room.

"Just a minute!" No more man-handling, no more being told what to do, no more stick-in-the-mud.

She was making it her job to unwind him by whatever

means necessary. And she did mean *whatever*. She wasn't her father's daughter for nothing.

He could just consider it an early Christmas present.

She called downstairs to the spa and made sure she and John were getting a couples massage, then adjusted her breasts inside her halter top, pushing them upward for maximum cleavage. Turning the door knob, she pushed open the connecting door. "Morning!"

He grunted from his spot at the table, never even glancing in her direction.

"Did you sleep good?" She crossed to the table and leaned over, pressing a kiss to his cheek before she took a seat. His cheeks turned slightly red underneath his tan. Good. Nice to see he really did have a pulse.

Tish proceeded to load her plate with fresh fruit and waffles, but John didn't answer her. "Well?"

"Hmmm?" He wouldn't look at her, just focused on his meal. *Maybe he wasn't a morning person?*

She tried again, slower this time. "Did you sleep good?"

"Fine." He cut off a bite of mango and forked it up.

"I slept fine, too. Thanks for asking." Tish slathered butter and warm strawberry preserves on her waffles. One thing she could say for John, he knew how to feed a woman.

They ate, the silence broken by the low chatter of news from the television. "I really think this spa day is going to be great," she finally said. "I haven't had one in ages."

John grunted in a way that made her fingers itch to slap him. Instead, she curled up in her chair, plate on her lap, acting as serene as possible.

"What *exactly* does Spa Day entail?" John finally asked. He sounded worried.

Of course, if she'd said Firing Range Day, he would have been on it like a hooker on free condoms. She finished chewing a piece of melon and licked the juice off her fingers, needing as much time as possible to act nonchalant. "Manicures, pedicures, a body massage, facial . . . whatever tickles your fancy."

"I'm not getting a manicure."

"Of course you are," she said brightly. "It'll be fun."

"Men don't get manicures." He spoke as if his masculinity was in jeopardy, and he'd do anything to protect it.

"Yes, they do."

He shook his head, his jaw twitching. "This one doesn't."

"Fine, but you're not getting out of the massage." And he hadn't said a word about the—

"No pedicures, either." He picked up his coffee cup "Nobody touches my feet."

Damn! "You're no fun."

"So I've been told."

True to her word, Tish didn't make him get a manicure or pedicure. But she refused to let him leave her sight. Which meant he was stuck in a chair next to her, reading a tattered copy of some girly magazine that advertised *proven techniques to achieve G-spot orgasms* and *how to find your man's erogenous zones*. John wasn't impressed.

"What do you think of this color?" Tish asked, holding up a bottle of polish.

"It looks like baby puke."

She snorted. "Like *you've* ever seen baby puke."

"Whatever. It's ugly." He should have brought a book, or maybe a sedative.

"Then pick one you like."

From her other side, Samantha giggled and sipped her mimosa. John was tempted to join her and indulge himself, but it wasn't even noon. On the other hand, some alcohol might improve his mood. Not to mention his day.

"Pick, John," Tish insisted, nudging the tray toward him. Tish Page was a complete and utter pain in his backside.

"I don't care."

She sighed, loudly and with lots of drama.

"You sound like an injured puppy," he said before he could stop himself.

From his other side, Mercedes, the brunette from the previous night, laughed and swatted his arm. She was tall with dark hair, a light tan, and enough cleavage to make a porn star jealous. She'd shamelessly flirted with him since he'd entered the spa with Tish this morning, seemingly oblivious to the fact he and Tish were allegedly together. Or maybe it was some sort of best-chick-friends game that he didn't get.

"Pick the red one," she hissed, pressing a champagne glass into his hand.

Against his better judgment, John didn't say no. He took a big swallow and grabbed a bottle of polish, setting it on the table next to Tish's hand.

"Ew."

"You asked me to pick. I picked." Smiling as the champagne hit his arteries and sped through his system, John flipped the magazine open.

"That's a great article." Mercedes laughed huskily as she tapped the page.

John glanced at the page, then downed the last of his drink before flipping to a new page. *G-spots.* He shuddered, unwilling to give Mercedes a reason to think he was actually going to read it. He knew all about G-spots and didn't feel the need for a refresher course.

She laughed again, louder this time. "You should get a pedicure. A foot massage would help you unwind."

"I don't like having my feet touched."

"Not even by Tish?" Mercedes countered.

"Not even by Tish," he echoed. His grip on the glass he held tightened at her reference to his sexual prowess. "I'm. A man. Men do *not* get pedicures and . . . stuff."

"Yes, they do," Natasha called out from across the aisle, interrupting him. "My fiancé does all the time. He was supposed to be here for spa day, but his flight from Miami was delayed."

Men who got pedicures. John shook his head. His choices seemed to be get drunk or stick a pointy manicuring instrument in his eye, but he needed his eyes. While the girls got their feet done, he nibbled on little sandwiches and sipped another mimosa, tuning out the women's chatter.

How many mimosas would it take to get him through that massage?

Against his better judgment, John undressed, carefully folding his clothes and leaving them on the bench in the miniscule changing room. Just like pedicures, massages just weren't manly . . . or dignified . . . or cool.

He double-checked the towel around his waist before stepping out of the changing room, which was barely big enough for him to turn around in.

His eyes met Tish's over the swinging door of *her* own changing room. She smiled and dangled her bra at him.

John squeezed his eyes shut at the mental image of her naked breasts, and other naked stuff, and turned his attention to the long, padded tables between them. The dimly lit room, the scented oils that permeated the air, and the piped-in sound of ocean waves didn't soothe John at all. Neither did the sight of Tish stepping through the swinging door wrapped in a towel that barely covered her ass.

"Nice." She grinned and wiggled an eyebrow despite the slight flush on her cheeks.

"You're a pervert."

He stretched out on the table, doing his best to keep his manly parts covered and not stare at Tish as the masseuses entered the room. He blocked out the visuals of Tish, with her creamy-pale skin (that was probably lusciously pink in all the right places), and reluctantly let his masseuse work him over. She kneaded and pummeled away knots he hadn't even realized existed, systematically liquefying his muscles and eroding all his earlier arguments about how unmasculine it was.

By the time she was finished, so was John. He was stuck somewhere just to the left of snoring. He barely registered her soft order to take his time getting dressed. Good thing, too. He wasn't sure he'd be moving anytime soon. Wasn't even sure he wanted to, until something nudged his consciousnes. A touch so light he thought, at first, it was a bit of oil trickling down his spine. But it was going up, not down. Electrical impulses followed, radiating outward and settling in his balls.

The table shifted and someone settled at the base of his spine. John's muscles were still too rubbery to move, his brain still too foggy, but *wrong* registered somewhere in the depths of his brain. This was wrong.

Soft slippery hands dug into his back, pushing their way up his spine. He moaned and shifted slightly, unwilling to unseat his companion despite the wrongness of it all. Then he felt it—er, them.

Breasts pressed against his back. Naked ones. And lots of warm slippery skin that teased a moan from his throat. The air in his lungs evaporated; his eyes flew open. He reared up and glanced over his shoulder, nearly unseating Tish in the process.

He wasn't normally slow, but on this one, his cock had beat

him to the punch, hardening while his eyes processed the visual in front of—on top of him: generous, pale breasts, taut pink nipples, flat belly, tiny shear panties, and a neatly trimmed snatch that hid her clit. The silver cross so close to her breasts. As he shifted onto his back, John licked his lips and swallowed the lump in his throat, ready to ask what the hell she was doing.

"Those are huge," came out instead.

She laughed softly and leaned over until they were nearly nose to nose. Her nipples dragged against his chest, stealing his breath and freezing his tongue.

"What—"

"I'm seducing you," she said, answering his incomplete question.

"Don't," he groaned. "Please." His cock was screaming at him to shut up and take it like a man.

Her hair tickled his skin, and her warm breath caressed his ear, while her tongue gently flicked at his earlobe.

"Tish."

She shushed him and nibbled at his ear again, tracing it with her tongue. Her hand slid between their bodies, tugging his towel open, caressing his cock.

This was bad. Very bad. He told her so, but she just laughed again.

"Condoms," he gasped.

His groin tightened and his cock throbbed, wanting release. His fingers itched to touch her, slide deep inside her pussy and make her climax. The image of him spurting come into her hands, in her mouth, filled his head, searing itself on his brain.

"Close your eyes."

He blinked instead, shaking his head. "We can't."

"Yes, we can." Now both her hands were on him and something cool and damp surrounded his cock. It roused him from his sexual stupor. "Lay back."

John finally pushed himself fully upright. "No, we can't."

"Gimme one good reason." She gently massaged his balls, rolling them between her fingers.

"Someone could come—"

"I know." She grinned wickedly and wiggled against him. "That's the point."

"Your dad," he choked out, hoping that would make her see reason, or at least, slow down. It definitely had a cold-waterlike effect on his cock.

"I won't tell."

"I would." He forced himself to back away from her, nearly falling off the table in the process. Two steps and he was in the dressing room, relieved to have some space between them.

"Why would you tell my dad?"

With shaking hands, John jerked on his pants. He yanked the zipper up, then reached for his shirt. He really didn't want to get into this with her. Not here; not now.

"Why?"

He jumped at the sound of her voice right behind him. If he told her the truth, she'd make the next few days of his life a living hell. Then again, knowing Tish, she would anyway.

He sat on the tiny seat and furiously yanked on his socks.

"John . . . " She pulled the door open.

He squeezed his eyes shut, searching for a way to evade her question and failing miserably. He was cornered by a naked woman who made him want to take advantage of everything she had to offer. The only way to stop her was to shock her.

"I can't lie," he finally said.

"What?" Her soft voice was filled with disbelief.

He licked his lips and forced himself to look at her. Damn, she was so pretty. And she was going to have a field day with this. "I can't lie, *okay*? Now, would you lay off? Please!?"

"At *all*?" Her face wrinkled slightly in confusion (and horror?). Her mouth formed a tiny O.

He nodded.

"Is it, like, some sort of genetic mutation?"

"No, no, no . . . it just *is*." Damn, explaining erections to his sister Dani had been easier. "Sometimes I can work my way around it, but I don't tell bald-faced lies."

She nodded slowly as she looked him up and down. "Like that shit about Natasha's ring being big."

"Exactly."

"Holy shit." Her lips curved into an amused smile.

Indeed.

This just got better and better. Momentarily distracted from her seduction, Tish crossed her arms over her bare chest. "How do you . . . do your job if you don't lie?"

"Long distance, mostly."

She snorted as some of her anger at John thwarting her seduction dissipated. She almost felt sorry for him. "So I could ask you *anything* and . . ."

"Please don't." He closed his eyes again, turning his head toward the wall. "I'm begging . . ."

"I bet that kinda sucks."

"You have no idea."

As days went, this one had turned out to be even more stellar than Tish could have hoped. She dabbed some perfume behind her ears and tweaked the diamond studs in her lobes. One last coat of gloss on her lips, and she was ready for dinner.

Tish knocked on John's door, jiggling her leg and waiting for him to open it. She was incredibly displeased at what she saw when he did: battered shorts and matching T-shirt. "You're not dressed!"

He stepped back and waved her inside. "Not going."

"You *have* to."

"Can't. Won't."

"Because of the—"

He nodded, looking almost as miserable as he had earlier. Poor baby. No wonder he was such a stick-in-the-mud!

She almost felt sorry for him, but not *that* sorry. "Look, John, sweetie, I'm sorry about the lie thing, really I am, but I did *not* come to Nassau to spend the entire time in a hotel room. Now get dressed."

"No."

"Yes, John." She pushed past him, her stomach rumbling at the sight of a perfectly grilled steak and glass of red wine on the table. God, she was so hungry! Ignoring it, she headed for the closet, thumbing through his clothes until she found a silky, pale yellow shirt that would compliment her multicolored sundress. She grabbed a pair of jeans off another hanger, turned and threw the clothes on the bed. "Get dressed. We're going out."

"Tish."

"No more bitching." She shook a finger at him. "And no more whining."

"This is a really bad idea."

"I can't go out without you. And besides, how bad can it be?"

"Yes, you can."

"Okay, well, I *won't*. And besides, it's just dinner and some dancing. How much trouble can you get into?" She crossed her arms over her chest prepared to wait him out. No way was she going alone, not when Vince was supposed to be there. He'd come in on the same delayed flight as the groom, one of his oldest friends.

The stare-off didn't last as long as she'd thought it would before he caved.

"More than you know." John yanked off his T-shirt, snatched the yellow shirt off the bed, and slid it on, covering the broad expanse of his chest. His eyes on her, he slid off the loose athletic shorts he'd been wearing and grabbed his jeans, stepping into them.

"I'll protect you." As long as he protected her, she would.

He shoved the tails of his shirt in his jeans and buttoned. "Thanks. I appreciate that."

"Sarcasm doesn't become you." This round went to her, but Tish was still determined to get Mr. Stuffed Shirt into her bed. Granted, she could understand why he didn't want to have sex with her, why he was so stuffy and reserved, and why he probably couldn't keep a girlfriend for very long even if he was super yummy-hot.

A guy who couldn't lie. It was like fat-free chocolate. And not that diet stuff with the nasty additives, but the real thing, just with all the calories zapped away.

She giggled as he stalked past her. He slammed the bathroom door behind him only to step out a few minutes later, his hair damp, his five o'clock shadow a thing of the past.

She held out her hand, pleased when he took it without a fuss. "Come on, Romeo."

By the time she finished her entree, Tish had almost decided to call it an evening. Her ex had arrived and spent the last twenty or so minutes throwing smirky looks in her direction. She hadn't kept John around to make her ex jealous, but for protection against Vicious Vinnie—her new pet name for him. He had a tongue like a razor and hadn't been afraid to use it in the few months since their breakup. Between the smirks and the third degree that the groom and assorted folks had peppered John with, it was shaping up to be a bad night.

As for poor John, not only did he not know anyone at the table—besides her—even general chitchat apparently had landmine potential for him.

Mercedes gently nudged her with an elbow. "Don't let them get to you," she whispered. Mercedes was the only other person who knew the truth about her breakup with Vince and about John, and she'd never tell.

"So John..." Kevin, the bridegroom, settled back in his chair, a bottle of Dos Equis in hand, his other arm draped over Natasha's shoulders, a smug expression on his face. "What do you do for a living?"

She liked Kevin, she really did, and he and Natasha were a good match, but he could be such a pretentious blowhard. He also took a lot of pride in his daddy's money and not much else.

"Family business." John motioned to the waitress to bring him another whiskey sour.

"Don't we all?" Kevin laughed, and the rest of the guys joined in.

Tish barely suppressed a snort of her own. Damn near every man at the table was involved in a family business, though some were more legitimate than others. She decided it was time to step in for the save. "John's... a spin doctor. You know, he makes PR nightmares go away."

"How long have you two been dating?" Kevin asked. The noise level among the groomsmen noticeably dropped, then immediately picked back up again.

"Since June." Vince had dumped her in May.

Kevin nodded slowly, studying them both like he wanted to ask more questions. But he didn't, thanks to Natasha, who'd started to pout.

John didn't say a word, and Tish hid a smile behind her wineglass.

With Tish's hand tucked in his, John reluctantly followed the boisterous wedding party out of the hotel and down the street to a nearby bar. He still hadn't recovered from dinner. Where the hell had Tish come up with *spin doctor*? He didn't even want to know.

"So, did you like it?" she asked softly so none of the others would hear her.

"Yeah, dinner was great." A blast even.

"I meant spa day."

He would never in a million years admit how much he'd enjoyed that massage, or the sight of her on top of him all but naked.

He puffed on his cigar, compliments of the groom, and hoped she'd drop it.

"You *did*," she purred triumphantly. She dragged him to a stop and stood on her toes, her lush body pressed against his. "You *liked* spa day."

He kept puffing, hoping the cigar wouldn't make him sick before she gave up.

"What was your favorite part? The facial, the massage with me, or *oogling* Mercedes's cleavage?"

He shrugged and turned away, opting not to answer, because it was a tough choice. He still couldn't believe he'd let her arm-twist him into a facial.

"Was it the cleavage? Are you a breast man, Johnny?"

He started coughing and threw the cigar in a gutter while Tish laughed. Apparently satisfied, she grabbed his hand and dragged him along the crowded sidewalk, hurrying to catch up with the rest of their party.

Inside the bar, almost everyone took off for the dance floor, leaving him to, once again, drown his misery in alcohol. The only thing that kept him on the island was the threat of pissing off Big Tom and, of course, his dad, who would probably disown John when he found out what he'd done; where he was. Tish had him by the short hairs. Sadly, a part of him was enjoying it. And her.

He watched her shimmy and shake with Mercedes on the dance floor, touching and bumping like two cats greeting each other. It seemed sort of fitting, he thought as he returned the tiny wave she gave him, then wished he hadn't when Tish broke free of the crowd and headed toward him. She grabbed his hand and tugged, ignoring his shaking head and the beer bottle in his hand.

"Oh, come on! I'll let you feel up Mercedes." She tugged again, her hand slippery in his. Her dress clung to her breasts and one of the thin straps slipped off her shoulder, giving him an eyeful of tit.

"I don't dance."

"Yes, you do. Everyone dances." She shouted to be heard over the music. "Now slug back that drink and move it, mister!"

John reluctantly slugged. He really, *really* couldn't dance, but lucky for him, being the meat in a Tish-Mercedes sandwich didn't require much on his part. They rubbed, they wiggled, they grabbed his ass and giggled, then dragged him to the bar for shots, and did it all over again. He lost complete track of time, his senses blurred by the loud music, sweat, and the sexuality that oozed off both women. By the time they let him come up for air, he was ready to become Tish's permanent love slave. And Mercedes's, too.

Especially that first time they kissed. Needing a chance to catch his breath and calm his... racing heart, John had just made his escape from the dance floor and downed a glass of water, only to turn and find both ladies wrapped in each other's arms. He couldn't stop staring, and somewhere in his mind it registered that Tish wasn't pushing Mercedes away or vice versa. No one around them seemed to have noticed or cared, except for a few of the groomsmen, who were nudging each other and laughing. They stopped, though, when they caught John's eye.

The duo exited the dance floor. Mercedes joined the rest of the group while Tish zeroed in on him, hiding at the bar—not that there was really anyplace *to* hide. Not from her.

She leaned against him, rested her chin on his chest, and licked her lips. "Like that?"

"Was that for me?" he countered. He couldn't bring himself to push her away, even though he knew he should.

She shrugged and pursed her lips. "Yes and no. Maybe," she added coyly. She studied him through thick eyelashes.

He swallowed, almost afraid to ask her what that meant. He eyed her lips as he wet his own. Tish's mouth curved into a smile, then she laughed. For some odd reason, it hurt the tiniest bit.

"You're playing with me."

"Yes and no." She leaned closer until her heavy breasts were pressed firmly against his chest and her hips were . . . well, there was no hiding his erection; she knew exactly the effect she was having on him. "Sweetheart, if I was playing with you, *you'd know it*." She nodded knowingly, one eyebrow quirked.

"Can we go now?" God, he needed a cold shower and about five minutes with his hand.

"Don't you want to dance with Mercedes and me again?" With her arms locked around his neck, she was so close he could smell her perfume, something crisp and strangely seductive that mixed with her natural scent.

Tiny beads of sweat clung to her upper lip. John wanted to lean down and lick them off. Just a few measly inches.

"Or maybe you'd like to see us ladies dance in private?" Despite all the drinking they'd done, her eyes were crystal clear.

Just because he *wanted* to didn't mean he *should*—or that he would. "Yeah. Now can we go?" If he didn't get out of here, he was going to embarrass himself or get them both arrested.

"Sure." Instead of leading him toward the exit, Tish dragged him toward the dance floor.

"Tish!"

"Come on." Tossing her hair over her shoulder, Tish kept walking. "It's a slow one."

More of *her* pressed against *him*. Luckily, *just* her. Mercedes was nowhere to be seen.

John wanted to say no, pull his hand free, and walk out of that bar. He knew if he did, though, she'd be pissed and, more important, he might never forgive himself if he passed up the chance to slow dance with Tish. She spun around and landed in his arms. John held onto her for dear life, his primitive male side happy to let her know what she was doing to him, that she'd probably be the death of him and, right then, he didn't care. She wrapped her arms around his neck again, and they swayed to some song he didn't recognize. Her body was angel-soft against his, as was the hair that tickled his jaw. It even smelled like apples, reminding him of their first meeting.

"You're really hot," she said.

John groaned, glad she couldn't see his face.

"You've got great hands." Her breath was warm against his ear, her voice seductive and soothing. "I was thinking about them last night. After you went to bed. I was thinking about those long beautiful fingers fucking me," she purred, tightening her grip. Last night, when he'd heard her masturbating. He wanted to tell her he'd listened but words failed him.

Her breasts were crushed against his chest. "And then today... during the massage, I kept wishing it was you... touching me, rubbing me. I kept waiting... hoping you'd slide a hand between my legs... play with my pussy. I wanted to fuck you so bad."

He squeezed handfuls of her ass, pulling her as close as possible in hopes of relieving the ache building in his balls and cock. "My God."

"I want you to fuck me, John." Her tongue tickled his earlobe, and his cock responded swelling and throbbing. All reason (and all his blood) had pooled between his legs. "And I know you want me, too."

Instinct took over. He locked an arm around her waist and dragged her through the thick crowd of drunken tourists into the muggy night air. It was dark and heavy, and John's ears rang slightly from the bar's loud music as he practically pulled Tish down the sidewalk. Foot traffic was lighter now, and he kept his eyes peeled until he found an alleyway that satisfied him. He dragged Tish into a recessed doorway, pinned her in place, and covered her mouth with his. She tasted warm and sweet, her plump lips soft against his, her curvy little body pliant against him. She kissed him back, her arms winding around his neck and tongue tangling with his until he finally came up for air.

"The hotel," she panted.

He reached for the hem of her dress, lifting it out of his way. "Too far."

4

Warm night air washed over Tish's skin, gentle as a silk sheet, as John pushed her panties down. She kicked them aside, whimpering softly as she struggled with his jeans. Her pussy was so wet, so swollen, it seemed to make all of her ache. "Touch me."

He did, one hand sliding between her aching lips, gliding past her clit and slipping deep inside her while the other helped her with his zipper. She moaned, wriggling against him, and almost gasped in relief when she finally freed his cock. He was hot and thick in her hand and didn't waste any time. He replaced his fingers with his dick and pinned her in place.

Tish clung to him, a part of her hoping no one found them here, the rest of her loving every deliciously nasty, naughty minute of it. The rest of her wanted to get caught, wanted someone to see them, to watch them. She threw her head back and arched into John, almost climaxing at the thought.

He held one of her legs up and pistoned into her. Aching and feverish, she moaned loudly and wriggled against him, her breath escaping in short bursts as she struggled to catch the orgasm that eluded her. She was so close she could taste it, but as usual, couldn't seem to get quite close enough, and then John moaned loud and long and it was too late.

Tish swallowed the thick ball of disappointment lodged in her throat and pressed her face against his shirt. She discreetly sniffled back her tears.

She'd really, *truly* wanted this one, more than any orgasm in recent history, including every one Vince had tried to give her, but once again, she'd missed the train.

Once their clothes were back in place, they didn't talk again until they crossed the still-busy lobby and reached the hotel elevator. Inside, John and Tish didn't touch, they didn't even look at each other until the two young couples they picked up on the second floor finally exited on the tenth floor.

"Have you ever slept with Mercedes?" he asked once the doors had closed and they were on their way again.

She rolled her eyes before she could stop herself. Maybe she should have dragged Mercedes with them. He'd probably like that. No, he'd probably end up feeling as threatened as Vince had. "No," she glibly lied.

"Never slept with a woman?" John softly asked.

"Sorry to disappoint you, but no," she lied again and didn't feel the least bit sorry for it.

"Did you come?"

"No," she snapped before she could think up a suitable lie. Maybe John was rubbing off on her. She shrugged as if it was no big deal and kept her eyes on the climbing numbers above the doors.

His fingers gently grazed her shoulder.

"It's no big deal." She shrugged and stepped away, wishing he'd stop touching her. She wanted a shower, her bed, and her trusty vibrator. Pedro never let her down.

He exhaled, and she risked a glance in his direction. He was smiling and smug—and damn his fucking hide, satisfied. "So Tish Page has an Achilles' clit."

"It's not funny." She threw a scowl in his direction before she could stop herself. Damn him, he'd hit a nerve. A big nerve-filled one.

"I didn't say it was."

"You didn't have to."

The elevator doors slid open, and she started down the empty hallway on shaky feet. She wanted away from him. She wanted a shower . . . she wanted . . . she didn't know what the hell she wanted.

John followed, watching her luscious ass shake underneath the thin material of her dress. Her underwear was still back in the alley. He smiled at the memory of their encounter. He'd never done anything like that; he'd never lost control like that; he'd never let a woman, or anyone else, goad him like she had. And he'd loved every hot, sweaty second of it.

He paused at Tish's door, waiting until she was inside. It slammed shut, echoing up and down the hallway as he continued on to his own room. Instead of heading for the shower, he stalked to the connecting door and listened, but didn't pick up on any sound or movement from Tish's room. John slid his keycard in the lock and turned the knob.

She stood at the foot of the bed wearing nothing but her beige strapless bra. Her smooth skin was marked only by the occasional mole, like the tiny one just to the left of her belly button, and her neatly trimmed pubic hair was dark, a sharp contrast to her pale skin and the tiny, pink bit of flesh that played peekaboo from between her cunt lips.

Instead of snatching up her dress and covering herself, she propped her hands on her hips. "What?"

He nodded, his body tensing in response to her casual nudity. "You do that a lot."

"Do what?"

"That hands on hips thing." He moved close enough to smell himself on her, and it made him hungry—*she* made him hungry.

She crossed her arms over her breasts as if she were covering herself. As if she'd finally been hit with an attack of modesty. "I was going to take a shower."

John glanced toward the bathroom; her purple vibrator sat on the vanity. "With that?"

"Yeah. Feeling threatened?"

He slowly shook his head, then waited to see if she'd give in first and break the heavy silence.

Sighing, she reached back and unhooked her bra. She tossed it aside and circled the bed.

He followed, seduced by her naked body, the jiggle of her ass, and her boldness. His fingers itched to pick up her dress, bury his nose in it, and see if it smelled like them, too. "Can I watch?"

She shrugged, drawing his eye to the curve and dip of her spine. "Suit yourself."

Smiling, he dropped her dress on the floor and trailed after her.

It took everything Tish had not to jump when the bathroom door clicked shut. And she felt like an idiot for letting John, of all people, push her buttons. Pretending he wasn't there wouldn't be easy.

She crossed the chilly bathroom floor to the oversized shower and turned the lever, hoping it wouldn't take too long for the water to warm. She wasn't exactly in the mood for small talk. Since she had some time to kill, Tish decided to take off her makeup—otherwise, by the time she climbed from the shower she'd look like a raccoon. She quickly brushed out her hair and gathered it up in a ponytail holder, hoping John wouldn't notice her shaking hands, then scrubbed at her face with makeup remover. Tish was acutely aware of John's close proximity—it was less than a foot from where she stood to the bathroom door—and her own nakedness.

Despite John's presence, Tish was determined to treat this like any other masturbation session. Five minutes, ten tops, then she'd wash up and go to bed—alone. She rinsed away the suds, then patted her face dry, her body warming as the tiny space filled with steam.

John still hadn't said a word.

Heart clanging against her ribs, she threw down the hand towel and snatched up her trusty friend Pedro, climbing in the shower with him. She reached for the shower door, only to have her hand stall as she made brief eye contact with John. She forced her chin up a notch and pushed it open, hoping the occasional burst of cool air wouldn't make this take longer than normal.

She turned her vibrator on, immediately noticing the normally soft buzzing seemed loud as a jackhammer tonight.

"Want some help?" he asked, moving closer to the shower door. His clothes were growing damp from the steam, and his shirt started to stick to him.

She lowered her eyelids and shook her head, dipping the humming vibrator between her thighs while warm water coursed over her body. Her pussy hungrily sucked it in while her clit, still tender from their encounter in the alleyway, throbbed with excitement. The energy shift in the tiny room was subtle. Tish's eyes drifted up the length of John's body, noting the outline of his cock along the way. Her eyes met his and suddenly, him watching her wasn't a bad thing. Her body tightened with anticipation, hips arched upward, and she slid the vibrator out, rubbing her clit with it.

He was gonna fuck her again. At least once. She watched through sex-heavy eyes as he moved closer. John kicked off his shoes and stepped into the shower. He wrapped his hand around the dildo and slid it deep into her pussy. He pulled it out, just long enough to tease her clit, then back in, fucking her. Tish braced herself against the tile wall. Him being there, doing the job for her, combined with the fingers that found her swollen clit and gently stroked her, sent her over the edge.

Her hips bucked while her pussy repeatedly clenched the vibrator. Finally, she sagged against the wall satisfied, spent, and shaken.

Eyes closed, she struggled to catch her breath and yet again, fight the urge to cry. Thank God for the shower.

"Turn around," John softly growled in her ear.

"I need a minute." She licked her lips, thankful when he didn't force her to spell it out for him. Instead, he wrapped his arms around her, cradling her against his wet shirt and stroking her back until she gave him a gentle nudge. She turned on shaky legs, arching her hips to give him better access, and sucking in a deep, noisy breath as he slid his thick cock into her.

For this round, he took his time; there wasn't an inch of her pussy his cock didn't explore.

Finally, he pulled her from the shower and finished in bed.

Tish had woken up to find John pressing little kisses on her shoulder blade. They'd snuggled, sleepily for a while, kissing and exploring each other's bodies as only new lovers could. John had to keep reminding himself that it wasn't real. It was just a game.

"Do you *want* to sleep with Mercedes?" John ran his fingers through Tish's hair, pushing it off her face.

"And you called me a pervert." She tried to wriggle away, but he wasn't having any of it.

He studied her for a few quiet seconds, then said, "You didn't answer the question."

"You just want to watch." She pulled the sheet up to ward off some of the chill.

"Maybe."

God, would he just drop it already? "You're *such* a guy, and don't even bother trying to deny it."

"So what's on the agenda for today?" What adventure was she going to torture him with? Though, after last night, he was feeling pretty mellow.

She rolled over and propped herself on his chest, smiling in a way that made him shiver. "Today, I'm going to teach you to lie."

"You're *what*?"

"I'm going to teach you to lie."

"Why? Wait, no! You're not. No, Tish. Absolutely not."

She rolled her eyes. "Get with the program. *Everyone* lies, John." She narrowed her eyes. "You've never told a lie?"

He swallowed the lump in his throat and stared up at the ceiling. "I guess. I probably lied as much as anyone else."

"What happened?"

"I told a hell of a lie, and it cost someone her life. Decided after that it wasn't worth it." The memory still made him sick.

"You're a hit man," she said matter-of-factly.

He nodded slowly, reluctantly, unwilling to say even to her that he tried not to think about his job. Or that it occasionally left a bad taste in his mouth. That he felt like a fraud because he was so good at what he did. "I wasn't then. I was in college, and my dad asked me to help a friend of his."

"It was a hit?"

He nodded and said, "I wasn't naive." Maybe he had been, or maybe he hadn't been as worldly as he'd thought. "I knew about my dad. His friends. Guns. I'd been raised around them."

"And," she softly coaxed.

"I got close to someone." He'd never told anyone this; not even his brothers. He'd done his best to forget. "On purpose."

"You set her up?" It was as much a statement as a question.

He nodded again, unwilling to say anything more about the matter, unwilling to look any closer than he already had. It was a door he wanted to shut and lock as quickly as possible.

"Would you quit . . . if you could?"

"I don't know what else I'd do." He snorted with laughter. "It's not like I could go into law enforcement, though I did try. You know what it's like." Being part of a family like theirs, where blind acceptance and obedience were expected. Wynn hadn't quit; Will had; John couldn't.

"My God, it's a wonder your dad didn't disown you!"

"It was touch and go there for a while." John smiled ruefully. "We still don't speak much. Not any more than we have to."

"You know, we can't be held accountable for our families. Don't get me wrong. We can say no, get out, try to lead a normal life, but it's not easy. *They* don't make it easy, and you just get so used to it."

"A part of me likes what I do, likes the challenge." He frowned up at the ceiling.

"So you kill from a distance," she said softly. She snuggled close and pushed his hair off his forehead. "And you keep everyone else at a distance, too."

"Yeah," he sighed. He appreciated the fact that she got it more than she knew. "Tish, I'm sorry about Mark."

"That's okay." She smiled at him. "You're a lot more fun."

* * *

They'd showered together, then hit their respective rooms to dress for the day. Other than "lying lessons," Tish didn't have a lot on her calendar until that evening—just the rehearsal and the dinner. Maybe they could get some sightseeing in.

He sat on the edge of the bed watching her smooth on her makeup. "Are you sure you can do this?"

"What? Teach you to lie? Puh-leeze! Of course I can." She flashed him a smile over her shoulder. "John?"

"Hmm?"

"Does my ass look fat?"

He glanced at her face. One eyebrow arched, she nodded her encouragement. He swallowed hard, his eyes traveling down her bare back. They came to a stop at her generous hips covered with a tiny black scrap of material. "I like fat asses."

"John!" A makeup sponge hit him in the forehead.

"Sorry. But I do." He eased to his feet and crossed to stand at the bathroom door. He set her sponge on the counter. "Not fat, just, well, like yours."

She lined her eyes with a dark gray stick before meeting his gaze in the mirror. "The most important rule of lying is: *Keep it Simple. Always* keep it simple. The more you explain, the more elaborate you get, the higher your chances are of getting called on a lie. Got it?"

"Got it."

"John?"

"Yes, Tish."

"Does my ass look fat?"

Unable to help himself, he glanced at her ass again. "Your ass is perfect." And that, at least, was the truth.

She snorted. "We'll make a liar out of you yet."

* * *

"I wasn't lying," he insisted for like the fiftieth time since they'd left the suite. "I really do like—"

The elevator doors slid open, preempting whatever he'd been about to say. Tish bit her lip, wanting desperately to laugh at his misery as an elderly couple joined them. They rode down to the second floor together, then ended up leading the way to the restaurant for breakfast.

She tucked her arm in his and squeezed his hand. "Relax. I believe you." Funny enough she did, but his misery was endearing.

"I don't think this is a good idea." He nodded to the waitress as they passed by.

"You'll be fine," Tish assured him. "Just remember to keep it simple."

She led him through the maze of tables covered with snowy cloths and gleaming crystal to where Samantha and Mercedes were sitting nibbling at bowls of fruit.

"Can't we sit alone?" he asked from behind her.

"No," she threw over her shoulder. "This is your chance. Just start small." She pasted a bright smile on her face. "Morning, girls!"

John pulled out a chair for her, then took a seat next to Mercedes, who grinned at him in a way that made Tish smirk.

"You two left early last night."

Tish gave him a pointed look—it screamed *lie*.

"Yeah," he said. "We did." He'd blown it and didn't care. He just . . . couldn't. He wasn't lying, no matter how hard Tish pushed him to.

He was saved from further comment by the arrival of their waitress. Once they had ordered their breakfast, he sipped his coffee, listening to the women chat about the previous night and the upcoming wedding.

"At least our dresses don't suck," Mercedes said.

"Have you seen Tish's? She got the best one." Samantha forked up a bite of Eggs Benedict.

"I did not."

"You did, too."

Samantha sighed and combed her fingers through her dark red curls. "I need a retouch so bad, but I ran out of time."

Even though his cup was still half full, John motioned to the waitress for more coffee and ignored Tish's arched eyebrow. No way was he talking about Samantha's roots. This was as bad as their earlier discussion about Tish's ass.

"Oh my God." Mercedes laughed. "Remember Renee's wedding?"

Tish joined in just as the waitress appeared with a small bowl of fruit for her and more coffee for him. "*Those* were ugly dresses."

"No, they were *fugly*," Samantha said. "Speaking of fugly, guess who got shitfaced last night? I mean, really shitfaced!"

"Who didn't?" John had just entered the sixth level of Hell, and he didn't even have any food to distract himself with.

Tish waved a dismissive hand in his direction, then turned her attention back to Samantha. "Spill."

A smug smile twisting her lips, Mercedes slowly leaned back in her chair. "Cari."

"Cari?" John said before he could stop himself. He'd been trying to tune them out. Cari with the curly brown hair, big brown eyes, and dimples—*dimples*!!

"Honey"—Mercedes laughed—"it's the innocent ones you gotta watch for."

"She left with two groomsmen." Samantha winked at him.

"Shit," he said under his breath.

"After she hit on Kevin," she added.

"Natasha?" Tish breathed, wide-eyed.

"In the ladies' room . . . lucky for Cari."

"Aren't you going to ask who she left with?" Samantha's grin could only be called smug.

Thank God he wasn't a woman. He'd never have survived puberty.

"No," Tish said, her focus on the fruit in front of her.

"Y'all going to tell Natasha about Cari and Kevin?" John asked as the waitress appeared with his eggs and waffles.

"Are you kidding?" Tish stared at him as if he'd sprouted two heads.

Samantha waved her fork in the air. "There are some things you just don't share."

John nodded slowly as he slathered his waffles with syrup. A lie by omission.

"She's getting married in one day," Tish added.

"Ever been around a bride so close to her wedding?" Mercedes asked.

"No." Never, thank God.

"Well, between the three of us, we've been in over two dozen weddings. Friends, cousins, old college roommates, you know." Tish shrugged.

"Brides are one Xanax away from becoming a homicidal maniac." Samantha forked up another bite of her eggs, reminding John that his were getting cold, but he couldn't hold back a laugh.

Tish glared at him. "We're not kidding."

He nodded, turning his attention to his breakfast. The ladies were anything but boring.

"That's so not fair," Mercedes grumbled.

"Huh?" He glanced at her.

"That." She nodded toward his plate. "If I ate eggs, waffles, and bacon for breakfast, I'd blow up like a balloon."

Another chance to lie. John could feel it slide right past him. He sighed. "Doubt it."

Tish snorted, while he sipped his coffee. What the hell *could* he say?

"That was reassuring," Mercedes quipped.

"Forgive him," Tish said. "He's a liar in training."

"Tish!" He scowled at her in shock.

The elderly gentleman at the next table cleared his throat and glared.

"A liar in training?" Samantha echoed with a giggle.

"Ho at twelve o'clock," Mercedes said from behind her coffee cup.

Cari had entered the dining room and was heading right for them. At least now they had someone else to snack on.

"Now's your chance, tiger."

Cari looked a little worse for wear, but not what he would have expected after a night spent with two of Kevin's groomsmen.

"Morning, Cari." He swiped a chair from the table behind them and held it for her.

"You're such a sweetie," she gushed even though her smile looked tired. Her makeup was sloppy, and she had stubble burn on her neck.

"Love the dress," Mercedes said. Whether it was a great dress or not, he couldn't say. Just like he couldn't say if Mercedes was lying.

Samantha smirked behind her coffee cup, and a red-faced Tish hid behind her breakfast; he did the same, wondering how much more of his day would be spent in hell. He wanted out of the restaurant and away from Tish's friends before he ended up in a catfight or worse. The ladies were interesting, but they were giving him a headache.

He was on his last bite of eggs when a harried-looking Natasha came rushing into the dining room, her breasts jiggling under her T-shirt and her hair sloppily piled onto her head.

She dragged a chair over to their table and collapsed dramatically. "Oh my God."

"What's the matter, hon?" Samantha pursed her lips in a way that made John think she was only being polite.

Maybe there was something to be said for honesty. He pinched the bridge of his nose.

"I need a drink," Natasha said.

John was probably the only one to notice how Cari subtly shrank away. Or how quiet Tish was.

"Mimosas." A grinning Mercedes raised her hand to catch the waitress's attention.

"My mom just called." Natasha slid lower in the chair and propped her head on her hand.

Cari relaxed the tiniest bit.

"Mimosa, please, and some toast with jelly. Lots of jelly. God." Natasha picked up Tish's extra piece of toast and nibbled at it until half had disappeared and crumbs spackled her chest. "How am I going to survive the next twenty-four hours with her around?"

He could definitely empathize. Hell wasn't hot. Hell wasn't filled with evil demons torturing you for all eternity. Hell was *this*: Being trapped at a table with five women, at least three of whom were hung over, and with no means of escape. He felt like his heart might give out from the stress.

Tish wanted to laugh at the pained expression on poor John's face. Instead she finally took pity on him and signed for their breakfast. She made to stand, but Natasha wasn't having it.

"You can't leave me. She'll be here any minute. Oh my God—" She slugged back half her drink, then squeezed her eyes shut as if she could wish her mother away. "She'll blow in here on a wave of Chanel and systematically ruin my wedding day."

"Why'd you invite her then?" John asked.

An obvious question but also a dumb one. Tish almost groaned while Samantha stifled a giggle.

"Hello! She's my mother! You can't *not* invite your mother to your wedding. It's just not *done*."

John got it; he did . . . but he didn't. "But you hate her."

"I don't *hate* her. She just drives me nuts. That's why she lives in Charlotte and I live in Atlanta."

"Your wedding coordinator has everything under control. I'm sure it'll all be fine." Tish gathered her purse, ready to try to escape again.

"At least she didn't bring her dogs," Natasha sighed.

"See," Mercedes chimed in. "There is a bright side."

A bright side, maybe, but Tish didn't blame Natasha. Her mom was a royal pain in the ass—emphasis on royal. And as much as she loved Natasha, the apple didn't fall far from the tree. She caught Cari's eye. And that shit about Cari and the groomsmen. Even though she'd said she didn't want to know who the lucky guys had been, Tish felt certain at least one had been Vince. Call it a hunch.

Not that she cared, but after the fuss he'd made over *their* threesome . . . she shook her head, then tried to smother the grimace she wore.

Tish finally stood, making calling motions at Mercedes from behind Natasha's back. "We'll see you this afternoon."

"Are you all right?" she asked John, once they'd left the women behind.

"I'll live, but I think I have an ulcer and scars."

Laughing, she slid an arm around his waist. "Was it horrible?"

"Horrible, yet educational." He draped an arm over her shoulder. "It made me want to hug my mom."

"Are you two close?" She wasn't one to normally feel like she *needed* protecting, outside of the bodyguard she'd grown so accustomed to, but she leaned into John, enjoying the oddly comforting feeling he gave her. She knew the Colliers by name—everyone did—but she didn't really *know* them. Their families seemed to run in circles that paralleled each other instead of intersecting; otherwise she might have made John Collier her business a long time ago. She liked him, really liked him. Her nipples tingled at the memory of him watching her in the shower, and how he'd shown his appreciation.

John pulled up short, and Tish realized she'd been so lost in thought, she couldn't even be sure he'd answered her.

"What day is it?" The expression on his face was pure deer-in-the-headlights as his grip on her shoulder tightened. Luckily, the lounge area outside the restaurant was empty because John looked as if his head might explode.

"Thursday—*ouch*." She shrugged away from him, breathing a sigh of relief when he let go. "Why?"

"I have to call my mom."

"Aw, how sweet!"

"If I don't call, she'll send out the cavalry. Never mind she doesn't know where I am. My brother does." He shook his head. "I don't even know where my cell phone is."

"Use the phone in the room."

"I don't want her to know where I am."

"Doesn't that kind of defeat the purpose of calling?"

John sighed. "I'm not sure, but if *she's* unhappy . . ."

"*No* one's happy," she finished for him, completely unable to hold back a grin.

He started toward the elevator.

"I'll come with."

"You don't have to."

"Yes, I do." She punched the UP button.

"You really don't."

The doors slid open revealing an empty elevator. No one was around; they'd have it to themselves. Tish dragged him inside, smothering the smutty ideas that presented themselves, and selected the button for their floor. "I'm coming along so I can help you lie to your mom."

"Lie—Tish!" He stared at her, a shocked scowl on his gorgeous face as he frantically shook his head. "No!"

"Yes! You'll be on the phone. You won't have to look at her. It's perfect!"

"Tish, I can't lie to my mother. I'll go to hell."

He was impossible, in a really sweet way that made her kind of warm and fuzzy. Tish smiled and grabbed his arms, turning him toward her. "We'll practice, okay? Now, make believe I'm your mom."

She made a pretend phone out of her fingers and held it to her ear. "Come on, play along!"

He rolled his eyes and made his own phone. "Hi, Mom."

"John! Wait, is your mother cheerful or grumpy or . . ."

He shrugged, looking confused as that crazed look he'd gotten on his face at breakfast returned. "She's *Mom*."

Tish rolled her eyes and picked up where she'd left off. "Hi, honey! Where have you been? You didn't call."

John licked his lips. "Sorry, Mom."

They stared at each other for a few slow seconds until the elevator doors slid open. With another roll of her eyes, Tish stepped out. She tried again as she led the way to her room. "Where have you been?"

"In the Bahamas."

"That was your cue to lie." She glanced at him over her shoulder, barely able to contain a laugh as she turned back to slide the keycard in the lock. "You didn't tell mama you were going on vacation. Are you having a good time?"

"I can't do this." John followed her into her room and closed the door with a groan of annoyance. She flopped on the bed and quirked an eyebrow at him.

"It's stupid."

"It is not. If you tell your mom you're in the Bahamas, she'll assume you're on vacation, right?"

He sank down next to her, his shoulders slumped.

"Aw, come on," she coaxed. "I'll trade you a blow job for a lie?"

"Don't you mean a lie for a blow job?" His lips twitched the tiniest bit.

"Whatever." She shrugged, her perky smile firmly in place.

"You don't have to do that."

"It's my pleasure."

"I can't tell my mom . . . What do I tell her? She knows I'm not working."

"Can you tell her you're at your brother's?"

"She'll ask to talk to him, so that's out—and she knows I wouldn't visit my sister."

"You have a sister?"

"Yeah, Dani," he replied absently. "Remember?"

"Uh huh. I always wanted a sister. What's she like?" All Tish had was an overprotective father and brother.

"A pain in my ass."

She giggled. "I'd love to meet her someday."

"You'd probably love her."

"Hey!"

"I meant that in a good way."

He eased to his feet. "I'm calling my mom and *not* lying."

"Okay, but I want to listen." Tish followed him into his own room.

He dug through his bag until he found his phone. "Why do you want to listen?"

"I just do!" Before today was over, he'd tell at least one respectable lie, or she'd know the reason why!

5

"Did she call?" Tish asked.

John was ready to shove her into her own room and lock the door. "Four times." He speed dialed his mom, then took a seat on the edge of the bed with his back to Tish. He appreciated her effort, he really did, but lying to Mom . . . "Hi, Mom! Sorry I forgot to call."

Lying to Mom was a huge no-no.

Tish angled around to stand in front of him, then proceeded to fidget and fret like a hooker in church.

"I missed you. I thought for sure you'd be home on Sunday for dinner," his mom said.

"Speakerphone," Tish hissed.

"Maybe next week." He tried to wave Tish off. What she failed to understand was that his mom knew about his . . . affliction . . . and spoke accordingly.

"Are you okay?" his mom asked.

He scowled at Tish's pouty face.

"Speaker," she hissed again.

He covered the phone so his mother wouldn't hear. "No."

"You're not?"

"Mom, no, I . . . the maid is here." His eyes closed of their own accord, and his head landed in the palm of his hand. Tish softly whooped and jumped up and down before climbing onto his lap. He'd lied and screwed up in the process. He held the phone far enough away from his ear so she could hear.

"Jonathan." Her sigh sounded disappointed. "I won't ask."

"I'll . . . see you . . . in a few days."

He hung up feeling as dejected as Tish was thrilled. The last person he'd wanted to lie to was his mom. Even a small lie. The experience left a bad taste in his mouth.

Her arms wrapped around his neck, a grinning, wiggling Tish pushed him back on the bed. "I'm gonna make you the best little liar in the whole damn world!"

Scowling, he pushed her off his lap. "That's not funny, Tish."

"I'm sorry." She shrugged almost carelessly, and she didn't sound sorry. She didn't look sorry, either. She looked . . . pleased.

Fine. Before the day was over, he'd wipe that smug expression off her face.

Even though the rehearsal and dinner were casual events, John had taken the time to press the wrinkles out of his black slacks and freshen the creases in the sleeves of his gray shirt. When Tish knocked on the door, he was ready.

She gave him a sultry once-over, followed by a smile meant to warm his insides. It almost worked. "You look very nice."

Saying she looked drop-dead gorgeous was the truth. Saying she looked like hell would blow his plan. Saying *nothing* would frustrate the hell out of her. So that's what he did. His lips twitched, finally curving into a genuine, full-blown smile. "Thanks."

* * *

The wedding would take place in a flower-draped pavilion surrounded by happy guests—or so said the wedding planner.

John stood toward the back, watching her try to move things along like a general herding rabid soldiers, all of whom seemed to have an agenda. Especially Natasha's mom, who looked too much like Natasha to deny *being* her mother. The older woman immersed herself in the thick of things *and* between the bride and groom as often as possible. Somehow, John managed to stay off her radar. He'd somehow missed the name of the mother of the bride, who purred and preened like a woman half her age. Kevin took it in stride; Natasha didn't—even walking out at one point. It took all the bridesmaids and the wedding planner a good twenty minutes to get her to come back. Smothering a laugh, John grabbed a quick scotch from the nearby bar. This beat reality TV by a mile.

For the rehearsal dinner three tables had been put together to form a *U*, so more friends and family could join them, and a bar and buffet featuring a roasted pig were stationed nearby. Sharply dressed waitstaff stood ready to slice, serve, and mix drinks. They had turned the patio into what amounted to an outdoor dining room complete with dance floor.

Tish came and slipped her arm through his. "Hope you weren't too bored."

"Of course not." *Lie number one—sort of.* John smiled down at her, ignoring the questioning look in her eye. He had been bored despite the entertainment provided by Natasha's mom. They stepped in line behind a stiff-shouldered Cari.

"Tish," an elderly voice rang out from behind them.

"Yolida!" She turned, dragging John with her, then released him long enough to hug the older woman. If she'd been at the rehearsal, John had missed her. Considering her turquoise ensemble and blond hair that clashed with her dusky skin, she would have been hard to miss.

"Is your father going to grace us with his presence tomorrow?"

"No. He said he was too busy to get away right now."

"Huh. I could have sworn I saw him earlier." She turned big twinkly brown eyes on him. "Who's your friend?"

Smiling indulgently, Tish introduced him to Natasha's grandmother.

"I can see where your granddaughter gets her stellar looks." He pressed a kiss to the back of her hand, while hoping he wasn't laying it on too thickly.

Yolida tucked her arm in his and nudged Tish out of the way. "I'm stealing this one."

John helped her through the buffet line, then carried her plate to a spot at the far end of the table. "Don't you want to sit closer to Natasha?"

"Yes, but unfortunately she's sitting near my daughter, and a bigger pain in the ass you'll never meet. Avoid her like the plague." Yolida motioned to a waiter. "Bring me a dirty martini."

As much as John really wanted to sit next to Yolida, who would probably be even more fun to chat with than Mercedes had been in the spa, Tish was making frantic "no-no" hand motions. "Enjoy yourself, Miss Yolida."

He carried his own plate to where Tish sat, with the bridesmaids and, of course, the bride and groom, who were positioned at the end of their table. John ended up sitting between Tish and Samantha. They were both drinking margaritas. As he sat down, he pointed to Samantha's glass. "Does that mean I should run?"

She giggled and patted his seat. "Depends on where you're running to."

He glanced down at the freckled swell of cleavage that blossomed from her dress, then back up, meeting her frank gaze. "You look stunning this evening."

From his other side came the sound of Tish sucking wind.

Samantha leaned closer and asked, "Are you lying?"

"Would I lie to you?" She *did* look hot, in a high-class call girl sort of way. Not that he'd *known* many call girls, but that was the illusion she gave off.

From the main table came the sound of shrill laughter. Natasha's mother was swatting Kevin on the arm and batting her lashes at him. Natasha, on the other hand, looked as if she'd just swallowed a tuna whole, and a few of the groomsmen tugged at their collars uncomfortably. "I take it that's the lovely mother of the bride?"

Samantha nodded. "She's adorable," she said, her words laced with sarcasm.

"*So* adorable," Tish added, leaning against his other side, "there's not enough valium in the world to keep poor Nat mellow."

"And what is that lovely vision's name?"

"Sally," Tish said.

"As in Mustang," Samantha added with a grin.

"That's an insult to Mustang aficionados everywhere." John turned his attention to his dinner. Antagonizing Tish was going to be much harder than he'd thought, and he needed fuel to make it happen—in more ways than one. More ravenous than he'd been in days, he polished off his dinner, then went back to refill his plate.

"Save room for dessert," Mercedes teased.

John turned and found her standing with Sally just a few scarce feet away. Behind a nearby potted palm, Natasha and Kevin were arguing while one of the groomsmen was deep in conversation with Tish.

A smart man—a sane man—would have walked away. Or better yet, run. John was still too mad at Tish to qualify as either. Decision made, he handed his empty plate to the waiter and moved toward the two women. "What's on the menu?" he asked, grinning down at the both of them.

Sally leaned toward him and gave him a smug smirk that left no doubt about what was on the menu. "Me, if you want."

"I'm afraid Tish would beat my ass if I even thought about cheating on her." It took everything he had to not laugh, but that didn't stop Mercedes.

Meanwhile, Kevin, who'd finally freed himself from Natasha and was working his way toward the bar, discretely made brow-wiping motions from behind Sally's back as if he was glad to be free of Natasha and Sally however briefly. Guess he didn't realize in twenty-four hours he'd never be free of either woman.

"And besides," John added, "Yolida already called dibs on me."

Mercedes snorted and gave a dramatic roll of her big brown eyes.

Tish was probably still talking and probably hadn't noticed he was gone. What the hell could she be talking about for so long? And how long was he going to have to stand here?

"Why would you want her when you can have me?" Sally motioned to her cleavage.

He shrugged, wishing like hell he could see Tish's expression. "I can appreciate an older woman."

She gave him a smoldering look from underneath thickly mascaraed lashes. Sally was a well-put-together woman who could have easily passed for her daughter's older sister thanks to some discreet cosmetic surgery and very expensive makeup. It was her voice that gave her away. He'd bet his favorite gun she was a long-time smoker, or had been at some point. "Excuse me."

He grabbed two pieces of cake and turned back toward the table, happy to see that Tish's friend was gone.

"Well, aren't you just the Casanova," she snapped before he'd even sat down.

So she had noticed. He forced the most innocent expression possible on his face and slid her dessert in front of her. "Whatever do you mean?"

"Flirting with Sally." She picked up her fork and stabbed the cake.

"And Yolida," he added.

"Who's next?"

"Maybe Cari." Ignoring her glare, he took his napkin and dabbed a bit of smudged lipstick from the corner of her mouth. "Maybe *you*. If you're lucky."

Ignoring the elbow she rammed into his side, John took a bite of cake that nearly melted in his mouth.

"You're mean," she hissed.

"I've been nothing but charming," he said as Kevin's best man stood up to make a toast.

The best man's eyes were on Cari, who looked amazingly hot in a low-cut orange dress, and he swayed slightly, probably due to too much beer.

John finished his dessert while the toasts continued, content to sit back and watch Kevin, Natasha, and Sally drink themselves cross-eyed, for reasons he could only guess at. Before the night was over, there would be another fight. Maybe two, if the constipated expression on Natasha's face was anything to go by. He debated whether he should say anything to Tish about her friend or keep it to himself until the band started.

"Where'd your friend go?"

"What friend?" she asked innocently.

"The one who kept you in deep conversation while I was getting you that cake."

"Oh... Vince." She picked off a piece of sculpted icing and slid it past her lips.

Apparently, John wasn't going to get any sort of explanation. He could have laughed except Samantha chose that moment to put her hand on his thigh.

"Where's my cake?"

He ignored her. "Vince... huh?"

He draped his arm over Tish's chair and smiled down at her even when she tried to pierce his thigh with her fork. He wrapped his other hand around her wrist and said, "That's rude."

"So is what you were doing."

"I like your friends. Doesn't that make you happy?"

"I hate you." Her cheeks flushed, she turned her attention to the ongoing toasts.

When her silence finally got to him, he leaned over and pressed his lips to her ear. "I was lying. Isn't that what you wanted?"

Before she could reply, he stood, thankful the speeches had come to an end. With a smile worthy of a barracuda, Sally leapt to her feet as well. John wasn't ready to wrangle with her yet. "Cari."

She blinked, wide-eyed, and stared up at him from her spot on Samantha's other side.

He stood and held out a hand. "Let's dance."

Out on the mini-dance floor, John said, "Do you have a boyfriend?"

She shook her head.

"You know Kevin's best man—"

She nodded before he could finish, her head dipping so he couldn't see her face.

Realization dawned. "He was one of the—"

"You *know*?" Her head shot up, her big, puppy-dog eyes filled with embarrassment.

This was one of those unfortunate times when lying would be downright stupid, and for Cari, even cruel. "Yes, but what you do is your business. I don't judge." Even if *her* lack of judgment had left him a bit surprised, he wasn't in a position to judge *anyone*. Especially taking into account his occupation and the fact he'd had sex with Tish in an alley.

Cari swallowed and wet her lips with the tip of her tongue. "I'm *so* stupid."

"We're all stupid, *often*. Do you like him?" *Was he really having this conversation?*

"Joe?" she wrinkled her nose, obviously reluctant to confess anything. Finally she gave him another tiny nod. "Yeah."

"So go talk to him." Women always had to make things so damn complicated.

"What do I say?"

" 'Hi'?" At the doubtful expression on her face, he added, " 'Are you interested in round two?' Or 'How about a walk on the beach?' " Shit, he sounded like Dear Abby . . . on crack. "What have you got to lose?"

This wasn't how he'd planned this evening. Time to get back on track, soon as he figured out what the deal was with Vince. "So, Vince?"

"Does it bother you being here with him?"

"No" would definitely be the wrong answer. "Kind of." God, Tish was gonna make a liar out of him yet!

"I can imagine. He and Tish were together a long time, and you're the new guy."

John was well-trained enough he didn't stop dancing and didn't stare at Cari in shock. "The new guy," he echoed.

"Yeah, you know. Coming in and changing the group dynamic. Vince, Kevin, and Joe have been friends forever, and Tish and Natasha used to be much closer, you know."

He nodded. When Tish was dating Vince.

"Their breakup kind of made things a little awkward."

"Especially with me here," John added.

Cari nodded and shrugged, almost apologetically.

He'd been played royally, and definitely had a bone to pick with Tish now.

Mercedes snagged him before Sally could, inching the older woman out by an eyelash, and before he could get to Tish, who was safe for now.

"I don't know what you're up to, or what you're pissed about, sugar, but you're playing a dangerous game. Tish isn't a woman you want to make angry."

"And I'm not a man she wants to piss off." He meant those words more than Mercedes would ever know.

"She's not very happy right now." She arched one delicately outlined eyebrow for emphasis.

"I can imagine." His eyes found Vince, who stood at the bar doing shots with one of the groomsmen. He was average... average height, average brown hair, average features. Maybe he had a hell of a personality. "Neither am I."

"For what it's worth, she seems a lot happier with you."

Cold, small comfort since they weren't really together. Wondering what it would take to really piss Tish off, he pulled Mercedes closer and gave her his most charming smile. "Do *you* have a boyfriend?"

She grinned up at him, obviously not as worried about her friend's feelings as she'd let on. "Are you offering?"

"Maybe." No, definitely not, but it was a fun game to play. There was no way he could keep up with a woman like her.

"You can't afford me." She laughed huskily.

"How do you know?" He briefly caught Tish's eye over Mercedes's head. Tish looked very unhappy, and she was next on his list.

"Trust me."

"Are you a kept woman?"

"Do I look like a kept woman?" she countered.

"Of course not . . . maybe." Grinning, he spun her toward her next victim and set off to see how much he could irritate Tish.

"What in fuck's sake are you doing?" Tish's Irish temper was about to go supernova!

"You do realize that made no sense," he countered almost smugly.

"Fuck you."

"Tish, *language*."

She totally wasn't buying that frown on his face. Tish crossed her arms over her chest. "Thought you said you didn't dance."

"You said yourself that everyone dances. And besides, who can resist Sinatra?"

"Figures." She grimaced, wishing she could work out what the hell he was up to. Between John and Vince, who'd been kind enough to ask if she was upset over his threesome with Cari and Joe, she'd had her fill of men for the evening.

"Can I ask you something?" John asked.

Sally was closing in on them. Tish took him by the hand and dragged him away from the bright lights and music of the party. She was ready to skip the wedding—best friend be damned—just to get away from John and Vince. They were both driving her nuts. And if John found out that Vince was her ex . . . John was no dummy. He'd put two and two together and be pissed as hell if he figured out that she hadn't just asked him to stay to save Mark or to be her bodyguard.

The sound of OneRepublic faded away, and the night closed in around them. A seductive and slightly humid breeze blew in off the nearby ocean, caressing her shoulders and nibbling at the edges of her temper. "Are you just going to ignore me all night?"

"I wasn't ignoring you." Lie.

She wasn't stupid by any stretch of the imagination. He was lying. "And what was that shit with Sally?"

"I was just being polite." Another lie. He was lying to *her*. Damn him! "John!"

"What?"

"Stop!" She cursed the dark that kept her from seeing his face. His fingers trailed up her arms to caress her shoulders. The tiny circles he drew in her skin made thinking about being mad at him nearly impossible. "I should never have taught you to lie."

Then his lips were on hers and she wasn't thinking of anything, except being alone with him here and the memory of what happened the last time they were alone in the dark.

His hands slid down her back to cup her ass and squeeze, then they were tugging her dress up. She pulled her mouth free and reached for his zipper. "Hurry."

His lips were on her skin, his fingers inside her panties, stroking her clit. She ground against him, unable to hold back a whimper. Her panties slid down her legs, whisper-soft. They tickled her skin and the sensation warmed her. She kicked them off, a part of her wondering how many she'd lose before this trip was over. Then he pushed her against the stone wall and lifted her leg. Cool night air washed over her naked skin. She exhaled raggedly as her warm, wet pussy stretched to welcome him. She struggled for air as he moved in time to the beat of the distant music, grinding into her while his fingers teased at her clit.

She sucked in another ragged breath, clutching at the rocks

behind her for balance. She didn't want to look at him, afraid if she did, she'd cry. So she focused on the velvety dark sky overhead until her impending climax rocked through her and she bit her lip to keep from screaming as he joined her.

Tish sagged against the wall, sucking in deep breaths of damp, perfumed air. John softly pressed his lips to her jaw, then her neck and her ear.

"You're amazing," he whispered.

She blinked and sniffled, forcing her eyes to focus on her surroundings. On him. Was he lying again? Tish wasn't sure she liked the monster she'd created. She didn't like knowing if he was lying and just placating her or if he meant it when he said she was amazing, and the question stung in some very vulnerable areas. "Do me a favor?"

"Hmmm, what's that?" He drew back and gently tugged her dress down.

"Stop lying." *Please*, went unsaid.

"I thought you wanted me to lie?" He slowly tucked his shirt into his pants and buckled up. His face was hidden in the shadows even though every once in a while Tish would feel his eyes on her.

From his bland tone of voice, she had no idea if he was laughing at her or not. She sighed and swallowed the lump in her throat. "Ready to call it a night?"

"We can't be rude," he said, offering her his arm.

Shit. She *had* created a monster.

Tish slipped inside the hotel via a side entrance and sought out the ladies' room while John went back to the party. By the time she rejoined him, Sally had him cornered, a martini glass clutched in her hand. It was a wonder she didn't have John's balls clutched in the other.

"Tish, I'm stealing him."

You wish, she thought, smile firmly in place.

"I told Sally she could only borrow me."

Sally now had an arm around John's waist, and only he, Sally and God knew where Sally's hand was.

"You owe me a dance," she purred.

Tish wanted to gag. Instead she turned away, searching the crowd for Samantha or Mercedes. The former was at the bar, doing shooters with one of the groomsmen. The latter was prowling the edge of the dance floor, champagne glass in hand.

Tish headed for Mercedes, then almost wished she hadn't when the other woman's lips curved into a knowing smile. No one would ever call Mercedes a fool.

"Enjoying yourself?"

Tish sighed, struggling not to roll her eyes. "Not really."

"Oh, come on. What's not to enjoy?" She motioned toward the dance floor, where Sally had John firmly in her clutches, and he didn't exactly look like he wanted or needed rescuing.

"You've got the beach and the moonlight and a hot man to snuggle with tonight after all these fools are done drinking themselves silly."

"Or at least whatever's left of him once she's through." Tish motioned toward the dance floor where John was dipping Sally.

"You are not jealous of Nat's mama?" Mercedes quirked a brow and pursed her lips.

Tish sighed and shook her head slightly. Of course not; she was just annoyed. "No." And tired of John punishing her. God help her, she never should have made him lie to his mother.

He'd made his point and then some.

"Put it out of your mind and go dance. Have a good time. Daniel's looking a little bored." Mercedes bumped Tish's hip, nudging her toward Kevin's younger brother. A law student, Daniel had missed most of the earlier festivities due to an internship, and he wouldn't give her shit about breaking up with Vince.

Daniel currently sat at a table for two, being monopolized by Yolida, who, frankly, would probably outlive them all. Vince was nowhere to be seen—thank goodness for small favors—and John was actually starting to look a bit . . . pained. Laughing, Tish waggled her fingers at him and strolled toward Daniel and Yolida.

Tish did her best to ignore John, who went from Sally to Yolida to Mercedes and then Natasha while she kept Daniel and a few other bored groomsmen entertained.

She finally caught up with John and Natasha at the bar.

"Thanks for keeping my mom entertained." Natasha smiled up at him.

"It was my pleasure." John sipped his whiskey sour and winked at Tish.

It was his pleasure to antagonize Tish all over again. Tish's gut, which had finally calmed to a simmer, reached a rolling boil all over again.

"Consider it a wedding gift." He drew Natasha's hand to his mouth and pressed her knuckles to his lips.

Tish clenched her teeth to keep her jaw from dropping open. That was laying it on thick, even for him.

6

"Stop it! Stop lying. You're driving me crazy!"

He grinned at her in a way that made her want to slap him, then leaned down and pressed his lips to her ear. "You look really fuckable in that dress."

Lord help her, she didn't know if he was telling the truth or not, but they had already fucked. She watched him walk away, wondering what sort of demon she'd unleashed on her friends. To her horror he headed straight for Sally.

Her heart pounding frantically in her chest, Tish followed, closing in just in time to hear him say, "You're as obnoxious as your daughter said you were."

Around them the crowd fell silent, then someone laughed softly. It was probably Mercedes. Tish bit her lip.

She reached for John's sleeve and tugged. "We should go."

"Why?" John turned toward her, that grin still in place. "Did I embarrass you?"

She stared at him, her face burning as the crowd returned to their previous noise level. "Yes," she hissed.

"Young man"—Yolida came swaying over, a beatific smile

on her face—"I'd marry you myself if I thought I could get you away from that one." She motioned toward Tish, who was busy wishing the ground would open up and swallow her and John both. Natasha would never forgive her!

"It's a shame your granddaughter is marrying an obnoxious blowhard," John said.

It was all Tish could do to keep from choking on her tongue while Yolida proceeded to laugh her ass off.

"Lord, ain't it." She patted him on his arm.

"I give 'em three years," John added with a nod.

"John, I like you better when you tell the truth," a laughing Mercedes joined their circle.

"I like you, too, but find a single man to fool around with, would ya?"

"The single ones can't afford me." She shrugged and a shadow crossed her face.

He looked her up and down. "Then buy cheaper shoes."

Tish tugged at his arm, praying he'd stop. Mercedes was her very best friend in the world. So what if she had a bad habit of using men. They'd done it to women for centuries!

Yolida was cackling so hard, she finally collapsed in a chair.

"Okay"—Tish stepped in front of him—"we're leaving."

"Good." He waggled an eyebrow at her.

"And you're sleeping alone."

"Yeah, right." He smirked.

Arrogant ass! She had to get him out of here before Kevin and the rest of the groomsmen found out he'd been shooting off his mouth.

She didn't speak to him again until they were in the elevator on their way up to the room. "I can't believe you!"

He struggled against the smile that threatened to break free. Tish still didn't have a clue. "What did you expect?"

"You were like a demolition derby out there. Jeez!"

He turned and leveled a narrow-eyed scowl at her. "*You're* the one who insisted I learn to lie." *Deal with it.* "What did you expect? I had a good teacher."

She flinched just enough to let him know he'd hit a nerve and turned her head.

"Just goes to show that getting what you want isn't always as much fun as you think it'll be."

Her head dipped, her bangs obscuring his view of her face, and suddenly, her attention seemed to be on the elevator's control panel. "Sorry," she whispered, then released a heavy sigh. "I shouldn't have insisted you lie to your mom."

Was she really as contrite as she acted? No telling with Tish. "You're a spoiled brat."

"I know." She sighed again, filling the silent elevator with the sound of it.

A part of him wanted to laugh and tell her to cut the crap. He wasn't buying her apology. Instead, he settled for a shake of his head—even if she couldn't see it. "I'll skip the wedding tomorrow," he said as the elevator doors slid open. Surely she could handle a few hours on her own, and it probably was for the best after what he'd said to Sally.

Her head shot up and she stared at him wide-eyed with what looked like fear. "Why?"

Was she kidding? "For starters, I insulted the bride's mother." He held the elevator door and motioned for her to step out, but she didn't move.

"But you *have* to go!"

"Tish."

Her mouth moved and finally words came out. "I don't want to go alone."

* * *

"Tish!"

"Please!"

"Go."

"Not until you say you'll go." Now she was pouting.

"Afraid Vince'll see you by yourself?" He leaned against the elevator door and crossed his arms over his chest.

Tish's jaw dropped, then immediately closed as she stood staring at him. Finally, she shrugged. "No."

Now who was lying?

"I think, under the circumstances—"

"Everyone was so drunk, no one's going to remember! Please, John! Say you'll go." Her lower lip rolled out the tiniest bit and, Lord help him, she looked like she'd burst into tears any minute.

"If I say yes, will you get out of the elevator?" He was tired, and a little drunk. He wanted a shower and then bed—with or without Tish.

She nodded, reminding him more and more of a five-year-old with her big eyes and pouty lips.

"If I say yes, will you tell me about Vince?"

She sighed, rolled her eyes, then, finally, nodded.

John found Tish sitting on his bed, dressed in a tank and PJ bottoms, her hair brushed out and falling over her shoulders, and her face free of makeup. He quickly toweled off and slid into a pair of boxers. After grabbing a bottle of water from the minibar, he joined her on the edge of the bed and waited for her to talk.

"We broke up." Her shoulders quickly rose and fell.

"No shit?"

She stalked across the room and got herself a bottle of water. "What the hell do you want?"

Cari's words came back to him. "You screwed up the group dynamic when you broke up, huh?"

"Yeah." She popped the seal and took a long swig, then delicately dabbed at her lower lip.

"Why?"

"I dunno. It's just a group."

"Why did you two break up?"

"What does it matter?"

She was too close to the door, ready to make an escape that John couldn't allow. "Come here." He patted the spot next to him.

"I'm fine. Besides there's nothing else to tell."

"Tish."

"I'm going to bed."

Tish stepped through the doorway into her own room. She almost escaped, but John was there, his huge body blocking the door she'd been trying to close. "John! I'm tired."

"It's barely midnight." He pushed, slowly forcing the door open enough to squeeze through, and then slamming it behind him. "Now, what happened?"

Tish crawled into bed, pulling the covers up to her chest. She set the bottle of water on the nightstand, all in an effort to stall for time. "In case you haven't noticed, I have a little problem."

He huffed, a smile teasing his lips.

"It's not funny!"

"So you and Vince broke up because you couldn't . . ."

"Climax. Come. Have an orgasm. Get off. Pop a cookie. Splooge."

"Splooge?"

"Yeah. I heard my brother call it that once." She frowned up at him, a part of her hoping like hell they were done.

"Who dumped whom?"

"What does it matter?" Please, God, drop it now.

"It matters."

"He dumped me."

" 'Cause you couldn't come?"

She hesitated too long. She knew it by the look in his eyes. "Yeah."

"And?"

"And nothing."

"Maybe it was him."

"And every other guy I've slept with—besides you," she added, waving a hand in his direction.

"I'm honored."

"Fuck you. Can I go to bed now?"

"What aren't you telling me?"

God, was she gonna have to take off her shirt to shut him up? "There's nothing to tell." Other than the fact Vince had begged her to have a threesome with another woman. Then he'd dumped her because she'd "enjoyed herself a little too much." Whatever... The threesome *had* been fun, but Tish was pretty sure she didn't play for the home team. She'd enjoyed sex with John too much for that.

"I don't feel like having sex." Besides, she was still a little tender from earlier.

"Did I ask for sex?"

"No," she grudgingly admitted.

He set his water bottle next to hers. "Do you know why you can't come?"

"What are you, a hit man or a therapist?" As much as she wished he'd leave, Tish made room in the bed for John.

He stretched out next to her and tucked one arm underneath the pillow. "Do you know why you can't come?"

"No."

"That's something to think about." He shut out the light and left her lying there in the dark, thinking. By the time she finally drifted off, she still had no answers.

Happily, John had plenty for her, in the form of some good, old-fashioned, morning sex.

"That was amazing." Tish threw one leg over John's and pressed her body against the length of him. She couldn't possibly have gotten any closer if she tried.

John ran his fingers through the silky length of her hair, trying to find a way to kill her post-coital glow as gently as possible. He'd been thinking about it all night, and as much as he'd like to keep seeing her once the wedding was over, there was still the issue of her cousin Mark. Dating her while trying to kill her cousin was . . . crass. "Tish, this has to end."

"Wow, you *really* know how to kill the afterglow."

"If your father finds out we've been sleeping together, I'm a dead man. And then there's that thing with your cousin."

She sighed. "Oh please, it's not like you popped my cherry. I'm a grown woman! And I don't even want to talk about Mark, so let's not."

John had a feeling her father wouldn't have cared if she was a virgin or not. She was his daughter. Enough said. Nor would he be as blasé as Tish about John ignoring instructions to stay away from Mark.

"We'll figure something out." A bare-assed naked Tish straddled his stomach.

"I dunno." Instead of climbing from the bed and gathering his clothes like he should have, John relaxed against the pillow, enjoying the view he was going to miss. "Your cousin; my brother. It's complicated."

"There has to be something we can do . . . *besides* say good-bye!" She ran her hands up the length of his chest. "You're the only man who can make me come."

"Honey, that doesn't exactly qualify me as Prince Charming."

"Maybe." She seemed pouty and lost in thought. "But I don't want to stop seeing you, John."

7

The wedding had gone off without a hitch, and nobody but Yolida seemed to remember his previous night's verbal vomit. Or if they did, they kept it to themselves. The reception was in full swing and John was seriously considering dragging Tish off for some good-bye nookie when someone tapped his shoulder.

"Mind if I cut in?"

The sound of Jimmy Page's voice froze John's blood—and the rest of him. He looked down at Tish, who stared back at him, eyes wide, her expression serious and a little scared.

He extricated himself from her suddenly clammy hands and motioned toward her.

Jimmy gave him a tight smile, then nodded toward the bar. "Dad wants to talk to you."

"Jimmy," Tish breathed. "What are you doing here?"

"Shut up, sis."

John didn't envy her a bit, but then, he didn't exactly envy himself either. He nodded at Mercedes, who threw him a little finger-wave, and wound his way through the tables toward the bar where Big Tom stood with Mark Green.

Even from this distance he could see that Mark was sweating. The oversized aquarium behind the bar glowed a surreal blue-green and cast a halo around Big Tom's bald head. He was about the same age as John's dad, but short and slight with a kindly smile and, dressed in a pale green shirt and dark slacks, he looked as threatening as tuna salad. "John."

"Sir." He stuck out his hand, praying the older man didn't notice how damp it was. Then he stared down Mark, whose glare was ruined by the tight-lipped fear underscoring his expression.

"Shoulda killed you," Mark muttered.

John snorted derisively and looked the shorter man up and down.

Tom's eyebrow twitched. "I see you met my daughter." He motioned toward the bartender, who quickly poured two fingers of scotch into a glass and slid it toward John.

He took the glass and muttered his thanks, a part of him wondering if it would be his last. Jesus, he hadn't been this scared since the first time he'd had sex.

"Don't you move, Mark." Tom started toward a tiny table for two, tucked into a softly lit corner, and John followed him, waiting to sit until after Tom was settled. He pulled out his own chair, discretely searching for muscle, guns, a prayer book.

"I only brought Jimmy."

Nodding, John finally sat. The presence of just Jimmy didn't reassure him, though he found it amusing that Big Tom didn't count Mark as muscle.

"This is a family matter." He sipped his drink, peering at John with sharp blue eyes. "And it needs to be settled once and for all."

"I realize I wasn't—"

The old man waved him off. "Mark's an idiot. Pure and simple. Takes after his father." He shook his head. "But you hunting him *can't* continue. I'm sure you understand why."

"Yes, sir." This was going nowhere good, and fast.

"Don't get me wrong. I respect a good, old-fashioned vendetta killing as much as the next man, but I also respect your father and your family."

"Yes, sir."

"And if I let you kill Mark, then I have to let Jimmy kill one of your brothers . . . or *you*." Big Tom gave him a pointed look. "It never ends."

"No, sir." He felt as if he was in junior high, sitting in the principal's office as he waited for the other shoe to drop. He knew Tom had a point; he was just taking his time getting there.

"What do you think of Tish?" Tom looked toward the dance floor where Tish and Jimmy were.

Oh . . . hell. John's fingers tightened on his glass. He now knew where Tom was going, and it wasn't someplace John had any desire to be. "She's something else."

The old man laughed. "She's a pistol. That's for sure." His gaze turned calculating as he refocused on John. "Did you sleep with her?"

He should have paid better attention to Tish's lying lessons. Much better attention.

"Never mind." Tom laughed again and motioned toward the bar for another drink. "I knew the answer when I walked in here and saw you two dancing together. She reminds me of her mother, but ornerier." He leaned forward, narrow-eyed gaze on John. "More important, she reminds me of *me*."

Nodding, John drained his drink and handed the empty glass to the waiter, who'd appeared with two fresh ones. He drained that one, too. If he was about to get smacked, and he was, a nice buzz would make it go down easy.

"You know what you have to do." Tom slipped a ring box out of his pocket. "I've already been to see your parents, and you have their blessing."

"Tish'll never—"

"Care to make a bet?" Tom laughed again and nodded to where Tish was sedately moving around the dance floor with her brother. "What do you think they're talking about out there? The boys of summer?"

She glanced at him but from this distance, John couldn't quite read her expression. He nodded slowly, resigned to his fate.

"That's a good boy." Tom slid the dark blue ring box toward John. "Now, go take your grandmother's ring and make this nasty business between you and Mark over, once and for all."

"If I agree to marry Tish"—John checked to make sure Mark hadn't left his spot at the bar—"he doesn't ever go after any of my family members again?"

"Ever," Tom said with a nod.

8

Tish watched John stuff something into his jacket pocket as he headed their way. "Jimmy?" Tish asked, looking up at her big brother.

"Marrying John is the only way to stop him from killing Mark. And besides, John's a good guy. He'll be a good husband. Or I'll kill him." Jimmy laughed, but Tish knew, when it came to her, he wasn't kidding. He'd beaten up her college boyfriend just for yelling at her.

"Mind if I cut in?" John asked.

Jimmy gave him a feral smile and released Tish's hands, stepping away so John could take his place. John, to his credit, didn't bat an eye.

"I'm sorry," Tish said.

"If you'd only let me kill Mark, we wouldn't be in this mess," he said with a laugh.

Tish couldn't hold back a giggle. He did have a point. "Unfortunately, Aunt Eunice would shit furry kittens if something happened to him." They danced quietly for the longest, slowest minute of Tish's life. "Maybe in a few years we can get a divorce."

Damn, her hands were sweating again, and it felt as if her knees were shaking, too.

John smiled and shook his head. "Divorce is too easy."

Tish stared up at him, shock coursing through her system. "Well, you can't kill me!"

He shook his head again. "I have no intentions of killing you. If I marry you, it's forever, Tish." They were halfway around the dance floor before he spoke again. "Now, if I get down on one knee and humiliate myself in front of all these fine folks, do you promise to say yes?"

Tish wracked her brain for something clever or witty, but came up empty, so she settled for the truth instead. "I have to tell you something first."

"What?"

Sighing, she glanced down at their feet, then back up at John. "I'm the one who told Mark you were here. So it's also kinda my fault we're in this mess."

He laughed softly and pulled her to the edge of the dance floor. "Guess you are like your father. Not that I'm surprised. Last chance, Tish. Will you say yes?"

"Absolutely."

Turn the page for a preview
of Kimberly Kaye Terry's novella
"Make Me," from
SATISFY ME TONIGHT!

On sale now!

Gideon's eyes drank in the sight of Tessa like a man lost in the Sahara, searching for water. The cheesy mental analogy made him wince, but damn if it wasn't true.

He forced his gaze away from her.

After a brief nod in acknowledgment toward Senator Waters, he turned his attention back to the small woman who lay on the narrow hospital bed staring at him. His hungry eyes went over her beautiful, angry face.

Her large, dark brown eyes widened as she stared at him, while the bottom rim of her wide, lush lips quivered slightly.

Nothing much had changed in her appearance since the last time he'd seen her close up, over seven years ago.

Her eyes gave her the appearance of a virginal innocent, completely at odds with the woman he knew her to be.

His gaze traveled down the short bridge of her nose and the nostrils that now flared in obvious anger and zeroed in on her lips. Her mouth was a perfectly shaped bow, like a present ready to be opened, he thought. He remembered a time when he'd been the first man to sample what her decadent lips promised.

Instead of the standard-issue hospital gown that showed a patient's entire backside, ass included, to the world, Tessa's small frame was wrapped in a scarlet red silk gown with narrow straps, the deep red striking against her chocolate brown skin.

Although most of her body was covered by the sheet she was snuggled inside of—that she'd brought all the way up to her chin, in fact, once he entered the room—Gideon already knew what the sheet hid from view.

LaTessa Price-Waters had a body built for sin.

After seven years, just looking at her sweet little body, even fully clothed and hidden beneath the thin, cotton, hospital-grade sheets and white throw made his dick thump in excitement and his balls swell in anticipation of getting next to her. He was soon forgetting the reason he was back in her life.

He willed his unruly cock to relax to no avail and kept his face neutral.

Now was not the time to take a trip down memory lane. Now was not the time to remember what it was like to be inside her, making love to her until they both lay sweaty and exhausted, unable to move.

Shit.

He'd come here, at the Senator's urging, to protect her before she got herself killed. Not that he needed the Senator's approval. Gideon had decided long before Senator Waters contacted him that it was time that he came back into Tessa's life.

With or without her controlling father's approval.

The fact that Waters had been the one to contact him and ask Gideon to actually *protect* his daughter, well, that was an irony that hadn't escaped Gideon's attention.

He quelled his knee-jerk reaction to seeing Tessa looking

vulnerable and hurt. Her pretty dark skin was ashen, and the small dark circles underscoring her eyes were prominent.

His first inclination, as he took note of the soft bandage that wrapped around her shoulder beneath her armpit and another small bandage placed above one of her finely arched brows, was to pick her small body up, haul her out of the hospital, and hide her from those wanting to harm her.

She'd come too damn close to being killed. Had he not tackled her to the ground seconds before the bullet hit, it would have landed in its intended target of her heart and she would have been dead instead of lying in the hospital bed, staring at him as though she were seeing a ghost.

"Gideon! So glad you're here. Maybe you can talk some sense into my daughter. God knows she's not listening to me!" Senator Waters exclaimed, obviously relieved that Gideon had interrupted what looked to have been yet another heated argument between father and daughter.

Gideon noted that, despite her surprise and obvious displeasure of seeing him, she shot her father an incredulous look. He bit back the unexpected smile when the Senator flushed under her penetrating stare. Nothing had changed between them.

No doubt Tessa wondered at the gall of her father to bring him back into her life, particularly as her father had been instrumental in removing Gideon in the first place.

"I don't know what is going on here, but whatever it is, you can forget about it! I don't need a bodyguard . . . protector . . . or whatever! I'm perfectly capable of taking care of myself."

"Why don't I leave you two to get reacquainted?" Senator Waters said to Tessa, ignoring her indignation.

After delivering an absent kiss on her furrowed brow, he quickly shook hands with Gideon and moved toward the door.

"What? Dad! I don't think so! Wait—" Tessa cried out, left

talking to the swinging door. Senator Waters had moved with admirable speed out of the room, giving his daughter no time to react to his leaving.

Smart man.

Tessa stared after her father, pulling the bottom rim of her lip between her teeth, the frown still firmly in place. She then turned toward Gideon.

Like a recalcitrant child, she crossed her arms over her chest and stared at him.

Unlike the child he likened her to, she had ample breasts, which were pushed up when she crossed her arms beneath them, and the upper, plump crests swelled above her gown. He tore his gaze away and, mimicking her, he crossed his arms over his chest and leaned against the wall near her bed and waited.

He didn't have to wait long.

"What the hell are you doing here, Gideon?" she asked angrily, barely getting the words out between her tightly clenched lips.

"You've been quite the... philanthropist... over the last few years, I hear," he said, purposely goading her, sliding his gaze lazily over her as she lay, covers deep, on the hospital bed.

He pushed away from the wall and walked closer to the bed until he was so close to her, he could feel the heat from her body reach out and caress him.

Unable to stop himself, he reached a hand out and stroked down the length of her soft cheek.

Her eyes stayed glued to his. Her mouth partially opened and soft breaths escaped as he allowed his finger to stroke down the line of her long neck, his touch stopping when he reached the bandages.

His eyes left hers and he stared down at the bandages. He lightly stroked his fingers over the white covering that wrapped around her shoulder and partially covered the swell of one of her breasts.

"God... you could have been killed, Tessa..." he murmured, inhaling a deep breath.

"Would it have mattered to you, Gideon, if I had?" she asked, with a hitch to her voice.

His eyes flew to hers.

There was a wealth of emotion in the depths of her dark eyes, ranging from pain to anger, before she closed her expression down.

But before she closed down, he caught the look of longing that had flashed in her pretty, dark eyes.

Her mouth tightened and she snatched the sheet even tighter up to her chin with one hand, staring at him malignantly.

If looks could kill, he was a dead man standing, Gideon thought in unease.

GREAT BOOKS, GREAT SAVINGS!

When You Visit Our Website:
www.kensingtonbooks.com

You Can Save Money Off The Retail Price Of Any Book You Purchase!

- **All Your Favorite Kensington Authors**
- **New Releases & Timeless Classics**
- **Overnight Shipping Available**
- **eBooks Available For Many Titles**
- **All Major Credit Cards Accepted**

Visit Us Today To Start Saving!
www.kensingtonbooks.com

All Orders Are Subject To Availability.
Shipping and Handling Charges Apply.
Offers and Prices Subject To Change Without Notice.